Hamilton Page

The Lady Resident

Vol. I

Hamilton Page

The Lady Resident
Vol. I

ISBN/EAN: 9783337047863

Printed in Europe, USA, Canada, Australia, Japan

Cover: Foto ©Andreas Hilbeck / pixelio.de

More available books at **www.hansebooks.com**

A Novel.

CONTENTS OF VOL. I.

CHAPTER XIV.

CHAPTER XV.

CHAPTER XVI.

THE LADY RESIDENT.

CHAPTER I.

CHRISTMAS AT HOME.

NORLANDS stands on the slope of a hill, about twenty miles from Westhampton. It is so large, so irregular, and so peculiar that it cannot fail to attract attention, though it is nearly half a mile . from the main road.

In the centre of a building which seems to wander at will over the hill side, there is a small two-storied house; and the only visible front entrance to the whole edifice is the door of this house; a small door painted green, with a brass knocker, and a porch of lattice work covered with roses and jasmine. A wooden balcony, festooned in the summer time by clusters of deep purple clematis, stretches across the upper windows;

and this central cottage is crowned by a high four-square, red-tiled roof, with a turret and bell on the summit of it.

On both sides of the cottage a lofty wing arises; irregular, many-storied, many-roomed, towering upward and stretching backward, reaching out into long low buildings, stables, dairy, laundry, tennis-court, vineries; losing itself in a kitchen-garden with borders of bright flowers and acres of glass. Even so the exuberant life of which this house is the garment cannot be restrained: it breaks out again beyond the bounds of the kitchen - garden in dove-cotes, pigeon - houses, rabbit-hutches, hen-coops, and sheds scattered over adjacent fields.

Twenty years before the date of this story Norlands was a small farm which Mr. Ravenshaw rented during the summer months for his young wife and her two children. The pretty cottage, fine air, and pleasant surroundings pleased them so well, that shortly afterwards, when it was offered for sale together with eighty acres of land, Mr. Ravenshaw purchased it.

He then resolved to leave the outer walls of the cottage untouched, to clear the inside for an entrance-hall, and to build his residence on both sides of it; the size and character of such residence to depend upon the requirements of his family and any fancy that might predominate at a given time.

Pursuing this plan Norlands had grown to its present dimensions, together with the owner's income, now very large, and a family that consisted of twelve children, the eldest a daughter of twenty-two and the youngest a *baby* of four years old.

Mrs. Ravenshaw always said that her tastes were simple. She liked a room to be perfectly square, and to have cupboards on each side of the fireplace, dwarf cupboards if it was a sitting-room, full-length if a bed-room, but in every case cupboards. The wall paper she liked with a white ground and plenty of it, and the Brussels carpet must invariably have a drab ground and be well covered with bright flowers. These points conceded, she left the rest to Mr. Ravenshaw and his whims. But Mr. Ravenshaw seldom conceded so much, and the rooms were of so many sizes, shapes, and modes of arrangement, of so many styles of architecture and modes of decoration, that it was a marvel how one roof could cover them all. Mr. Ravenshaw was a man who liked to carry out his ideas, and when he had a new idea with regard to the house, he built a room and embodied it. Perhaps it was on this account that friends used to say the great charm of Norlands was not so much its variety as its capacity. There seemed no limit to the numbers that could be entertained in it, as there was none to the hospitality of the entertainers. There was a warm welcome for old friends because they were old, and for the new because they were new. The twelve children were never without a sprinkling of cousins who wanted country air, or horse exercise, or archery, or shooting, or new milk. The elder boys and girls had each at least one bosom friend, chosen outside the family circle, and to be included in it as often as possible.

The house was always full, but on Christmas Eve ten years ago every corner of it was occupied. A merry troop of young people had been busy all day long with wreaths of holly, ivy, and laurel, with mottoes, banners, and devices, with ladders and hammers. At eight o'clock in the evening they were dancing in the hall as lightly and merrily as if the dance had not been preceded by twelve hours of work.

The sound of music and the hum of voices penetrated even through the double doors which shut off the dining-room, where a young girl was writing at one corner of a long table. She lifted her head from time to time as the sound of carriage wheels and a shout of welcome announced some new arrival.

The dining-room was long and low, with large windows and deep embrasures. At the end farthest from the door an enlarged copy of the old-fashioned farm-house kitchen chimney stretched from side to side of the room. The red-brick hearth was raised above the floor, great logs of wood burnt on it, benches of black oak stood against the walls, and the overhanging chimney-piece stretched in a long, low line across the room. It was of stone carved in many a quaint device, whilst the wall above it was paneled with old stamped leather and adorned with fantastic groups of helmets, swords, shields, and miscellaneous pieces of glittering armour.

Along the stone ledge there was now a motto with letters formed of ivy and holly leaves:

EAST OR WEST, HOME IS BEST.

So the young people had put it to please the father; whilst, to please himself, he had bade them add: "Chatted food is half digested."

He sat there in his favourite seat, the chimney corner, in a large arm-chair on the red hearth, with a Turkey mat at his feet, a table at one side, and on the other a little oriel window, from

whence in the day time he could see the garden
and his children at their play.

From time to time he laid down the *Times*
which he was reading and looked at his daughter.

She was copying a German song, saying the
words half aloud as she traced them carefully in
cramped German characters :

> "Der Vögel Sang verstummt im Hain,
>   Und öd' ist Berg und Thal :"

she murmured, and at the sound of her own
voice tears fell and blotted the page.

She did not discontinue her work, but took a
piece of blotting paper, absorbed the tears in a
very business-like manner, and continued writing.

"Won't you go and dance, Bertie ?"

"No, thank you, father ; I don't—— "

She could say no more, for the tears sprang
afresh. Her father looked at her in silence as
she quietly wiped them away.

> "Doch ist vom Glück was ich geträumt
>   Auch jede Spur verweht :"

she said, and went on with the copying.

Before long the door was opened, and in the
midst of a great burst of sound, a grim female
servant appeared.

"Miss Bertie, your ma sent me to ask if you'll
come and play a quadrille ?"

"Say I'd rather not. I am busy:" replied Bertie, with a flushed face.

There was another rush of sound as the maid retreated, and then a long unbroken silence.

Bertie's father rose and approached the table. He walked feebly, as one out of health and scarcely able to support the massive frame which nature had assigned him. He stood for a moment before his daughter, and his lips trembled as he saw the tears stealing down her face and dropping on the open page.

"Bertie," he said; and she looked up. "Bertie, my child, do you think your mother and I like to see you unhappy?"

"Oh, father!" was all the girl replied, as she rose and threw her arms round him.

"Now, my dear girl, don't cry."

"I won't, daddy; indeed I won't. But you see I can't be happy. I have tried as hard as ever I can, and really I can't be happy."

"Ah, well. I see how it is, and it's of no use to say any more about it."

"Don't be angry with me."

"No, no. I'm not angry; but I suppose wilful woman must have her way. When do you want to go?"

"To go, father! Where am I to go?"

"Well, I thought we'd wait till to-night; give you a month, and then, as you haven't changed your mind, I suppose that I must."

"What do you mean, father dear?" says Bertie, getting white. "Do you mean that I may go to college?"

"Oh, it's a college! Well, you shall go for a year. But mind, I only promise one year."

"But, daddy, do you really mean it? You're not making fun of me?"

"No; I'm earnest enough; and pretty work I shall have with your mother. Eighteen years old and going to school! Ah, well!"

"Father, dear, it's a college."

"Oh, it's a *college!* Caps and gowns, I suppose. However, my dear, if it's to make you happy you shall go."

Bertie could not speak. She kissed her father again and again, and he told her he would not be cried over. She said that he was crying also, and tried to prove it; and then, with both hands clasping his arm, she led him back to the arm-chair and sat on the stool at his feet.

The merry dance tunes resounded through the house. They could hear the tapping of the dancers' feet, and the clear ringing voices of the children at their games; but Bertie was too much absorbed in a discussion as to the comparative educational value of mathematics and logic to bestow any attention upon the trivialities of a Christmas festivity.

At length she drew a deep breath, and said almost with a sigh : .

"Father, I shall never forget this night. It is the very happiest time of my whole life, and to think it should come when I had given up all hope !"

"Never give up hope, Bertie, it is a bad habit ; and if you acquire it in youth you will go grumbling and doubting all through life."

"But what am I to do now when there is nothing left to hope for ? I have got everything I want. What *shall* I do, father, what *can* I do to show you how grateful I am ?"

"Well, my dear, I think you may as well try and do something that will please your mother. Go and show yourself in the hall. You can either dance with your peers or play with the children."

Bertie's face clouded. She was not prepared for such an immediate and distasteful form of gratitude. She thought her father might have asked her to read a chapter of John Stuart Mill, or at any rate that he might have allowed her to stay with him.

But he did not acquiesce in her views; she rose somewhat reluctantly:

"I may come back, father, mayn't I?"

"You may, Bertie. I shan't run away from the old corner."

Something in his tone arrested the girl.

"Oh, daddy, I do wish I might stay with you this one night. They are all so foolish with their dances and games and stupid jokes. I am so tired of it all; and I do think grown-up people should be reasonable."

"You are a very superior young person, my dear; but that has nothing to do with the matter in hand. You can try to please your mother; if you don't succeed in pleasing any one else you must not allow yourself to be discouraged by early failures."

Bertie's response was a blush and a hasty exit.

She entered the gaily-decorated hall in which the dancers occupied one part and the children another, although just at that time the two parties had joined in a game of forfeits. The front door opened into this hall, and on either side of it a fireplace, in which a large fire burned brightly, showed where the parlours of the old farmhouse had been. A broad staircase ascended from the centre of the hall and led to a gallery which surrounded the four walls. That part of it running along the front of the house communicated by means of glass doors with the wooden balcony already noticed ; whilst on the other three sides numerous doors, long irregular passages, steep and winding stairs, led to the rooms in the two wings and the adjacent premises.

The gallery was gay with Chinese lanterns and Christmas devices. The young people ascended the broad staircase and walked round it between the dances, much tormented by children playing at hide and seek, and darting in and out of doors and passages. Some of the elders of the party sat there looking down at the gay scene below them ; but the majority of these were in the two drawing-rooms and the library, which were on the opposite side of the hall to that from which Bertie entered. On this occasion the drawing-rooms were given up to whist tables and the library to bagatelle, whilst in the hall, when Bertie entered, forfeits were being called.

She walked towards the nearest fire-place, and a voice called out :

" Bow to the wittiest, kneel to the prettiest, and kiss the one you love best."

Bertie looked on with an expression that

seemed to say she was prepared on this occasion
to tolerate much folly. A young man with light
hair, and a clean-shaved, pale, and rather cada-
verous countenance, came forward and went
gravely through his bowing and kneeling, amidst
merry laughter caused by the deliberation and
anxious thought he seemed to bestow upon the
matter. When these preliminaries were concluded he approached Bertie without a trace of
irresolution. She stood with one hand on the
mantelpiece, and as he came forward their eyes
met. In hers there was a sudden startled look
which arrested him for a moment; then with a
slight smile he stept forward and kissed her on
the cheek.

She did not speak or move, but stood erect,
quivering, and with a face from which every
trace of colour had fled. Young men standing
in groups eyed her keenly, some of the girls
laughed, the elder sister approached and said:

"I wouldn't stand and look such a tragedy
queen, if I was you. Fred is only like your own
brother."

Almost at the same moment a little dark-eyed
woman, round and merry, bustled forward with a
look of great concern:

"Oh, Bertie, dear, you mustn't mind it; it's

all a childish affair. It is very foolish and wrong
of Fred, and I shall give him a good scolding.
Come with me, my dear:" and she took the
girl's hand and led her from the room.

Fred meanwhile looked uncomfortable. He
turned round and said with the tone of a person
aggrieved: "Why do they play at such absurd
games if girls don't like them? How should I
know Bertie would mind?"

"I tell you what, my dear fellow," said the
man addressed, who was some years older than
Fred, "a man is a fool if he kisses a girl before
he knows that she *will* like it. He thinks she
won't mind, and kisses her; then he finds out
that she doesn't like it. Just imagine what the
poor devil must feel!" and he turned away.

Fred was left to his own experience, which
showed that such a one would feel uneasy. He
waited for an opportunity of getting out unnoticed; and when the hall door next opened he
passed through it and walked up and down in
front of the house.

Bertie had returned to the dining-room. He
saw shadows on the window-blind, and knew that
his mother was with her. He walked backwards
and forwards before the house, and took out a
cigar. It was very awkward, he thought, for a

man to offend the girl he wanted to marry, on
the very night he has decided to propose to her.
Bertie had always been a curious girl, he knew
that ; but he had never doubted that she or any
other woman would be delighted to discover his
intention to make her the mistress of Elmsdale.
She ought to have known he was in earnest and
not to have stood there like an injured princess,
every one in the hall looking at her. He had
meant the kiss to be a suitable prelude to the
offer of his hand and fortune, and he was prepared to lead Bertie to the gallery and there
make known his magnanimous decision. Indeed
he had put two chairs in the embrasure of a
window, and had been waiting for her appearance
with some anxiety. When she came at that very
moment he thought the forfeit almost a provi-
dential interposition in his favour, and was proud
of his inspiration to kiss Bertie as the one he
loved best. Everything had gone against him.
It would be impossible to ask a girl to marry you
whilst she was angry, even though the offer was
such a good one. Perhaps Bertie thought he was
not in earnest. That was the thing. He had
never given any intimation of his preference, and
so she had misunderstood him. Well, that could
soon be set right. He would go to Mr. Raven-

shaw and ask permission to solicit the honour of
Bertie's hand.

The phrase pleased him. He said it over and
over again to himself, and thought that it might
well atone for a kiss. His mother might tell all
her friends that he had solicited the honour of
Bertie's hand. That would make it all right;
indeed his mother was sure to have made it right
with Bertie already.

When he had finished his cigar he re-entered
the house and went to the dining-room. Bertie
and her father were in the chimney corner, talking and laughing.

"I have come," said the young man, in a
solemn and rather pompous manner, "to request
the favour of a short interview with you, Mr.
Ravenshaw."

"Very glad to see you, Fred, if you are quite
sure you are not wanted to kiss any more young
ladies."

"Oh, father," said Bertie with a hot blush.

"It is not every young man," continued Mr.
Ravenshaw, "who has got the courage and presence of mind to kiss a girl in a deliberate public
way as they tell me, Fred, that you have done."

"Well, sir—," said Fred.

"It may be well, though I am not prepared to

concede so much; but I am told the kissing
would have been confined to the children if it had
not been for you, Fred, and even now your per-
formance isn't looked upon as a precedent."

"I beg, sir, that you will say no more about it.
I think you misunderstand me."

"Oh, we are quite ready to overlook it this
once, aren't we, Bertie, especially as it is Christmas Eve?"

"I must request, sir, that you will grant me a
private interview before you allude to the subject
again. I wish to explain my motives."

"Motives, indeed! Well, Fred, I always
thought you were not the kind of person to be
mastered by an impulse. Bertie, my love, I
can't leave the fireside; will you run into the
smoking-room whilst I hear these motives?"

The young man was not encouraged by his
reception, but neither was he discouraged. Mr.
Ravenshaw, so he often told his mother, was
always trying to snub him; but he was sustained
by the calm certainty that all he did was right,
and did not need the encouragement or consola-
tion which his mother was at all times ready to
offer.

Still there was just a trace of hesitation in his
manner as he stood opposite to Mr. Ravenshaw,

who smoked uninterruptedly, and looked steadily at him.

"He's a conceited, ugly, ill-conditioned dog;" was the thought that passed through the mind of his intended father-in-law : "I should like to see Bertie when she gives him his answer."

"Well, Fred, what is it you want?"

"I want permission, sir, to pay my addresses to Bertie."

"Oh."

"I suppose you have no objection, sir?"

"Why should I?"

"I thought not. You see you know me and my means and position."

"Uncommonly well. I have known you and your affairs since you were seven years old, just nineteen years ago."

"And are you prepared to support my suit:" said Fred, who was beginning to regain confidence.

"Can't say that I am, my boy; but I am prepared to support my daughter. If Bertie likes the proposal you can let me know. She's in the smoking-room."

"Then with your permission I will join her."

"Do so," said the father.

He left the room, and Mr. Ravenshaw watched him with a grim smile:

"He won't come out with quite so much manner as he goes in," he said to himself.

"Well, my love, what do *you* want?"

This was to his eldest daughter, Lizzie, who had darted into the room and was about to leave it.

"Oh, papa, I have come for Bertie. She really is *too* disagreeable. If she won't dance she might play for us. Mamma says she is to come, and I am not to go back without her."

"Come here, Lizzie, and I'll tell you a secret."

"What is it?" said Lizzie eagerly.

Her father pointed to the smoking-room door.

"Now, papa, don't tease me, for I've no time, and I'm not in the humour for it."

"I have been asked," he said, in a mysterious whisper, "for the hand of one of my daughters."

"Oh, papa, who is it?"

"Not you, my love. I said the eldest ought to go first; but it's of no use—"

"What a shame, papa. What do you mean?"

"Hush, my dear; not so loud. There's a young man in there on his knees to Bertie."

"She's a horrid little flirt," said Lizzie with a burst of tears. "I wonder you don't see through her."

"I do, Lizzie, I do; and I propose to send her off to school for a year."

"She'll get whatever she wants, I have no doubt of that :" retorted Lizzie angrily.

"It's a kind attention on your part, my dear, to tell me so."

"Well, papa, I didn't mean to be rude."

"That's the thing, my love; your condition is hopeless. You are rude without knowing it."

"I did think no one would quarrel with me on Christmas eve," sobbed Lizzie; "what with one thing and what with another, my life is a perfect wreck."

After a pause she asked,

"Who is in the smoking-room?"

"At present, my love, it is Fred Wilmshurst."

Lizzie turned away and left the room, and at that moment Bertie entered. Her cheeks were flushed, and her eyes looked larger than usual. She walked resolutely up to her father and said,

"Father, isn't it a disgraceful thing for a man to ask a girl to marry him in such a way?"

"In what way, Bertie?"

"Why, as Fred has done. He says he knew I didn't love him, and he glories in it."

Suddenly the girl flung herself down before a chair and covered her face with her hands.

"Oh, father, he thinks he can buy me, even me."

CHAPTER II.

HUSBAND AND WIFE.

"I DON'T like the plan. I never shall like it," said Mrs. Ravenshaw. "Bertie's head is full of nonsense, and she will be worse than ever if you encourage her and sanction her absurd notions."

"I do not sanction anything absurd; I never did."

"Now, Mr. Ravenshaw, you must confess that it is absurd to send a girl to school when she is eighteen years old, and has an eligible offer of marriage."

"Which she has refused."

"Many girls refuse a first offer. If she goes away now there is an end of the whole thing. If she stays, and Fred has opportunities of making his way, the result may be very different."

"I see no use in discussing a problematical result. My word is already pledged to Bertie;

and six months ago you agreed with me that unless Bertie gave up her wish to go to St. Mary's we had far better allow her to do so than keep her at home to pine and fret."

"Yes, Mr. Ravenshaw; but I agreed because I thought she would change her mind before Christmas."

"I don't think that alters the case. Bertie goes for a year only. Neither you nor I approve of very early marriages, and when she returns she will be only nineteen."

"But Fred may change his mind."

"I shall be glad to give him an opportunity of doing so before marriage."

"You talk in such a foolish way, Mr. Ravenshaw. Very few men with seven daughters would send the first that is likely to make a good match out of the way."

"My dear, you have always told me Bertie had no chance whilst her sisters were unmarried. Lizzie is twenty-two; she is the one who ought to marry."

"Lizzie has too many admirers. A girl with many lovers is slow to marry, and I cannot spare my eldest daughter."

"Well, there is Gladys. She is twenty."

"Gladys will marry a title, and we must not

precipitate matters. With her beauty we may
well wait a little."

"I don't want any of my girls to leave me;
but my dear little Molly is nineteen."

"Mr. Ravenshaw, this is a very unprofitable
discussion. If you have made up your mind
about Bertie, of course I must submit, and I beg
you to spare me your reproaches."

"Submission, my dear, is the strong point of
your character; and a woman who knows how to
yield is in the end always victorious."

"Then Bertie stays at home?"

"No, no. As you justly remark, we may very
well spare one out of seven daughters, and I
would rather send her to St. Mary's for a year
than to Elmsdale for a lifetime."

"Depend upon it we shall regret the step.
Bertie will never be satisfied with home life.
We shall lose her, without the satisfaction of
knowing that she has a good husband and a
good home of her own; and you begin to spend
money on education when she is out of the
school-room."

"It is impossible to foresee what the future
may bring forth to a girl like Bertie. I am not
very fond of strong-minded females; but, I must
confess, I should like to give Bertie a chance, and

see what she will do with it. Really when I find
what the education of the boys costs, it does seem
impossible to refuse the one girl who asks for it,
an advantage which she can obtain at so small
an expense.

"I never can follow your crooked reasoning,
Mr. Ravenshaw; but mark my words, Bertie
will marry; that's what she will do with her
education."

"Well, perhaps she couldn't do better."

"Of course she couldn't. But, after all the
trouble and expense we have already had, she
might just as well marry upon French and
German as upon this new-fangled Latin and
mathematics."

"Too late, my dear, too late. There has been
a mistake with Bertie from the very first. She
ought to have been a boy. A fourth consecutive
daughter has no place, even in such a large
family as ours. If George had preceded her as
he ought to have done, my eldest son would be
eighteen. Bertie would be fifteen; in the school-
room; no anxiety to Fred Wilmshurst or any
one else."

Mrs. Ravenshaw rose to leave the room:

"If you have nothing to say but such nonsense as that I see no use in talking."

"There is no use in talking," said Mr. Raven-shaw, "the thing is done."

The door was opened again and Mrs. Raven-shaw returned :

"I have only one thing to say," she resumed, "and it is this; you have done exactly what you liked in this house, and tried experiments all over it, from the garret to the cellar. There are not two rooms alike anywhere, or two stoves that burn on the same principle. Now if you are going to begin in the same way with the children I protest against it from the very first."

"My dear, don't excite yourself. The boys won't want to go to St. Mary's, and there is no fear of the three elder girls."

"I should hope not," said the mother angrily.

"Well, as Nelly is only eleven, and girls are not admitted to St. Mary's under sixteen, we shall have plenty of time to consider the subject of female education before her turn comes."

Mrs. Ravenshaw sat down and took out a handkerchief.

"Now, Jem," said her husband, "don't fret about it. Let the girl go for a year. That is all I have promised. Suppose it is a whim of hers and of mine too, haven't you always said that my whims made a happy home."

"Yes, John; but then they were not whims about the children."

"My dear, you forget; but never mind. Say it is a new whim of mine and give in to it like a good soul."

Mrs. Ravenshaw wiped her eyes.

"If I must, I must; but you will see that no good—— "

"I absolutely forbid a prophetic utterance," said her husband hastily, as Bertie entered the room.

"Bertie, go and kiss your mother. It has cost her a great effort to yield to my wish for you, and I know you will do everything in your power to show your gratitude and affection."

Bertie advanced with some hesitation, and her mother looked at her with a shade of anger, not unobserved by father and daughter.

The kiss was not altogether a success. Mrs. Ravenshaw put her handkerchief in her pocket, saying, "Well, well!" with an air of resignation as she rose for the second time to leave the room.

"Don't go away just yet, my dear. I want you to write one or two letters for me. We will make all arrangements at once, and then Bertie will be ready for the new term at the end of January."

Bertie's eyes danced with joy, and she had much ado to refrain from expressing her delight.

A warning glance from her father told her she had better leave the room. She would gladly have remained, but she saw that her mother was in no mood to allow her to be present. Moreover, it was all settled; when once her mother had yielded everything was sure to go on smoothly, no obstacles would be raised, and there would be no unnecessary delay.

Mrs. Ravenshaw took great pride in her business faculty, nothing pleased her so much as to be told that she was a capital woman of business; and Bertie, as she sat at the hall window looking out at the large flakes of snow falling softly on the bare branches of the trees or collecting into white masses on the shrubs, knew that her mother was making plans for her journey, deciding where and with whom she was to live, and what pocket money she was to have.

On all these points Bertie would have liked to express her views, but she knew the thing was not to be done. Moreover, she was really to go to St. Mary's! That was the main point, and her thoughts wandered away to the life and work which she had so often tried to picture to herself.

CHAPTER III.

GOOD-BYE TO THE CHILDREN.

THERE was much comment on this decision of the parents in favour of Bertie's wish. The elder sisters laughed; the elder boys, George and Charlie, home from Rugby, and Herbert from Wellington, said it was "awfully jolly," and the five younger children looked at Bertie with amazement and said nothing.

As the time drew near for her departure these five, with whom she was a special favourite, resolved to give her a treat.

"Now what shall it be?" asked Nelly, a girl of eleven.

"I think keeping shop will be best:" suggested Maggie, who was six. "We can get some raisins and biscuits, and cook will let us have the scales if we say we are going to weigh out plums for Bertie."

"Maggie, how greedy you are:" exclaimed

a third girl of eight years old. "You always want a shop because there's something to eat in it."

"What a story, Ethel!" pouted Maggie.

"I know what I'll do:" piped Leonard the youngest, and Bertie's especial darling: "I'll dwess Donald with wibbons and put on his new tail that Frank made him yesterday, and Bertie shall have him all to her own self and take him wound the hall."

"Oh, Lenny, Bertie wont care about your old horse."

"Yes, she will; she's very fond of him, and she shall have him all to her very own self. I won't even hold the weins."

The little fellow, who was sitting on a large wooden horse, much battered and curiously painted in spots and stripes, rose and patted it.

"Lenny, you might let me have Donald for a little, just to take him round the room."

"No, I shall not, Maggie. You pulled off his tail last time and hurted him."

"I didn't really, Lenny. It came off of itself. I only just put my hand on it."

"You pulled it off, Maggie."

"No I didn't, Lenny."

" Maggie, you pulled it off."

" You two always begin to quarrel when we want to talk," interposed Nelly; " now if you don't make it up at once you shan't join in with us."

" Well, but Lenny won't let me have Donald, and isn't it very selfish of him ?"

" Be quiet, Maggie. Now listen, all of you; shall we dress up and act a charade for Bertie ?"

" Oh yes, yes :" was shouted on all sides.

" Nelly, may I wear a gold crown ?" said Lenny.

" And may I be a cook and make some cakes ?" asked Maggie, " they bake beautifully on the hob."

" I'll be a schoolmaster," said Frank, a boy of ten years old who had not yet spoken, " and I'll have a cap and a black gown and a stick. Lenny and Maggie can run away, and then I'll flog them."

" Oh !" said Lenny, jumping about, " that's jolly; but you musn't weally hit, you must only pretend. And Jip may come in, because he'll bark when he sees a stick and make such a jolly wow."

" Trissy says you're not to say ' jolly row,' Lenny."

"It's holiday time, Maggie, and I shall say whatever I like. Jolly wow! jolly wow! jolly wow!"

"Hold your tongue, you naughty boy!" exclaimed Maggie, running after Leonard.

There was a struggle and a loud cry. ·Nelly interposed and scolded them both:

"You two can never be together without quarrelling, and I don't think we shall let you act in the charade at all."

"Well, Lenny will say *jolly row*, and he oughtn't to."

"What business is it of yours? Can't you leave him alone?"

"Now what are you crying for, Lenny?"

"She bited me:" said the little boy with a piteous face.

"Oh," groaned the three elder children with unanimous disapproval.

"I didn't bite, you naughty boy; you know I didn't," cried Maggie with shrill tones. "You put your fingers in my mouth, and you're a naughty boy, and I'll tell mamma."

"Now they are both crying," said Ethel in dismay, "and if Lizzie hears it she'll send us to bed directly after tea, just the very night we want to sit up."

"Leave off crying, Lenny," said Frank, "and go and ask mamma if we may dress up to-night."

Lenny dried his eyes, and seizing the leather reins of his horse dragged it away; the children listened as he clattered along the passage.

In a few minutes child and horse re-appeared. "Yes, we may; yes, we may:" shouted Lenny.

"And stay up to supper?" asked Maggie.

"I didn't ask; I didn't ask."

"Oh you are a silly; mamma would have said yes, and now we shall be packed off with a piece of bread and butter."

Maggie retired to a corner to sulk; whilst the other children, from the lowest shelf of the school-room cupboard, drew out a tumbled heap of stage properties and discussed their plans.

Bertie sat with her father on this last evening at home.

"May the children come in at six, father, and act their play?"

"Yes, if they get out of the way by dinner-time."

"Don't you know there is no dinner to-night. It is Lizzie's birthday; so there's supper at nine."

"So much the better for the children. Let them come by all means."

"They'll only have you and me for an audience, for mamma is busy with the maids. Lizzie wants the floor chalked in honour of the occasion."

"Pray how is Lizzie on this eventful night?"

"Oh, much as usual. Full of mystery and tragedy, and horribly cut up because there is no lobster salad for supper."

"And where is Gladys?"

"Gladys has got a new black net dress, looped up with poppies. Just now it's hanging over a chair before the glass, and Gladys is standing behind it to arrange the folds and puffs. Won't she look well in it?"

"Can't say. What has become of Miranda?"

"Dear old Molly. I saw her set off with a lantern and a pail. She is taking a bran mash to the pony."

"Your mother says it's time to leave off Molly, and call her Miranda."

"No, indeed, father; it can't be done. Molly wouldn't like it. She says she always thinks of the cows and the milking-pails when we call her Molly, and that is what she likes best. Here come the children."

A motley crew entered.

"What does the drawing-room hearth-rug represent?" asked Mr. Ravenshaw.

"It's the story of Red Riding-Hood; and that is Lenny, he is the wolf."

"What is the boy with the stick going to do?"

"That is Ethel. She always likes to be dressed like a boy. Frank is the grandmother. Don't you know we have to change the story for Lenny. He can't bear anybody to be eaten up; so Ethel has a big stick and rescues the grandmother first, and then little Red Riding-Hood."

At this point there was a loud cry; the grandmother had inadvertently trodden on the paw of the wolf. Lenny let the hearth-rug slip off, and sat down on the floor with tears streaming down his face.

"Oh, Lenny, you mustn't cry on Bertie's last night:" said Ethel; "and I'm so sorry. You know I didn't mean it."

"Pinch it hard," exclaimed Frank. "Pinch it as hard as ever you can; that's what the boys do at school; and then you won't feel the pain."

"Let him say what he'd like to do best:" interposed Nelly with an air of authority; "and then if he won't cry he shall do it."

"What would you like best, my pet?" said Bertie, who had taken the little fellow in her arms.

Lenny made a valiant effort to keep down his sobs, and at last said :

"May I be the appawition of a child ? "

"What does he mean ? " asked Bertie.

"That's his part in the play ; please let him do it, Bertie."

"Papa didn't hear it.   You know he was ill in bed when we had the play, and you were with papa all the evening, so you haven't seen it either, Bertie."

"Papa, may Lenny do his part in the play ? "

"By all means.   I shall like to see it."

Frank took the little fellow from Bertie and carried him out of the room ; Nelly followed.

A few minutes later the door was partly opened, showing a small figure and a little white face draped in a shawl.

A high voice with the tremulous tone of tears piped out :

"Macbeth, Macbeth, Macbeth, be bloody, bold, and resolute."

"Oh you darling ! " exclaimed Bertie.   "Bring him here, Frank, and let papa kiss him."

"No, no, no," shouted all the children.   "He can't come in, Bertie ; it would spoil everything. He's got to disappear.   The book says so.   He disappears."

"Very well. When he has quite done disappearing you can bring him to me:" said the father.

"He ought to say something more," interposed Maggie, "but he never remembers it."

An hour later the children were sitting at the dinner-table, and Maggie's bright eyes were roving over the dishes.

"I *am* glad there's supper," she said.

Bertie presided at the feast, and the children drank her health in lemonade and wished her a pleasant journey, each one adding in turn: "And, Bertie, will you write to me first?"

Lenny did not like to hear of Bertie's going away. He began to draw down his upper lip, and finally set up a piteous cry.

At that moment Mrs. Ravenshaw entered the room.

"Now, Bertie, what are you saying to that poor child? It is very cruel to hurt his feelings. Crying is so bad for him. Look at his poor little white, miserable face; I really am ashamed of you all. Come to mother, my darling, come away to mother."

"Now, mummy, don't be tross," said Lenny, who had an indistinct notion that Bertie was being scolded and he must take her part; "don't be tross, mummy. You said we might sit up, and *I* ordered the supper."

"My precious child. But who has been making you cry?"

The little fellow looked wistfully at Bertie.

"Nobody," he replied stoutly. "I *like* Bartie to go to College. I WANT her to go, and I sant cry again."

The two little hands clasped her neck so tightly that Bertie had to loosen them as she kissed him.

"Dear child," said his mother, "I think you ought to be an example to your sister. Bertie, I have come to tell you that you must start at seven to-morrow to catch the mail train, so you need not dance to-night if you don't wish it."

"Thank you, mother; I would rather not dance."

"Your brother George will see you to the train, and I have just had a letter from your uncle Harmer to say he will meet you at Exeter. You can stay all night with aunt Ellen, and the next day your uncle will take you on to St. Mary's."

"Thanks, mother. I will go and say good-bye to everybody before the festivities begin."

"Bertie, Bertie," shouted the five.

"All right," she replied. "I shall come and kiss you all in bed."

"Hurrah!"

Bertie danced from room to room, had just one waltz with the boys, admired Gladys, scolded Molly for being late, and was received by Lizzie with emotion.

"I did think, sister, you would have spared my feelings on this day. It is hard to say good-bye, perchance for ever, on my birthday.

"Nonsense, Lizzie. Why I shall be home in June, and nothing ever happens at Norlands. You'll all be just the same. The Pigotts will be coming, and Luke Hatherleigh, and the Caldecotts, and there'll be a dance; only it will be summer and the doors and windows will be all open, whereas now they are all shut."

"Ah, Bertie, you have no deep feelings."

"Lizzie," said Harry, bursting into the room, "Joe's come back."

"Well!"

"He's got the lobsters."

"Sister!" said Lizzie, turning to Bertie with streaming eyes, "it is a trifling matter, but you don't know how pleased I am; the supper would have been to me a *blank* without lobster-salad."

CHAPTER IV.

THE HIGHER EDUCATION OF WOMEN.

In the year 1862 the Professors of the University of Minster, moved by the urgent advocacy of two or three of their number, resolved to establish classes for ladies.

The scheme met with considerable approval, and Minster afforded it a rare combination of advantages. The staff of Professors, the prestige of the Western University, and the presence of a society remarkable for culture rather than for wealth and fashion were all in its favour.

The wives and daughters of Professors, the widows and families of many of their predecessors, and a very large contingent of unmarried females of all ages, gave promise of an inexhaustible supply of students.

Moreover, many of these persons had " connections," and there was an implied sanction of the scheme on the part of the church, the army, and

the bar.   Deans were not uncommon in Minster,
and Bishops not unknown ; general officers fre-
quented the place, and a Lord Chief Justice had
honoured it with his presence.   All these things
were taken as an indication that in Minster, if
anywhere in Great Britain, the experiment of
providing for the higher education of women
might safely be tried.

At the expiration of two years Principal
Ellice and Lady Mary his wife held a drawing-
room meeting to review the work done.   The
classes which had been carried on in the town-
hall had been so well attended, and the pecuniary result was so satisfactory, that it was
unanimously resolved to establish forthwith,
under the auspices of the Principal and Professors, a College for Ladies.

At this point numerous difficulties began to
crop up.   There was no endowment for such a
College, there were no funds, there were no suitable premises.   Persons who had recently founded
scholarships and contributed munificently to the
building fund for the enlargement of Minster
University drew back in dismay when it was proposed that they should establish a College for
Women.

A special dread of demoralising and pauperising the parents of girls was developed in all such, and they asserted that as an earnest of their sincerity those persons who advocated the higher education of women should pay for it.

The difficulties attending the undertaking threatened to be insuperable ; but after much patient effort Lady Mary Ellice called a meeting of the Professors and announced that they had been overcome. Two widows, Mrs. Milner and Mrs. Armstrong ; three spinsters, Miss le Mesurier, Miss Ellen Green, and Miss Julia Spiers, had resolved to contribute each £200 ; she herself proposed to add £500, and this sum of £1500 would be offered as a loan to the governing body of the College for Women.

She also announced that Mrs. Armstrong, Miss le Mesurier, and Miss Ellen Green had purchased from the creditors of Mr. Lumley the extensive buildings and large grounds known as St. Mary's Hall, where Mr. Lumley had failed to establish a remunerative school for boys. They had bought this property, a great bargain, and were willing to let it on agreement for three years at a very low rent.

Lady Mary Ellice proposed that the £1500 should form a guarantee fund, to provide for the rent, the execution of repairs, and suitable furn-

ishing of the college. The subscribers expected
no interest for their money until such time as the
college could afford to pay it ; but, at the suggestion of a legal friend, they asked that the furni-
ture and fittings should be secured to them.

Great was the rejoicing at the good news Lady
Mary announced. The six Founders, as they
were called, were the most popular women in the
city and had everything their own way. All
preparations were entrusted to the three pur-
chasers of St. Mary's, who were henceforth
denominated the managing ladies, or the managers. Principal Ellice and the professors, together with some ladies and gentlemen of good
standing in Minster, formed the governing body
or General Council ; and certain members of this
council were nominated to form a Ladies' Committee.

Three months later *St. Mary's College for
Ladies* was opened with all the pomp and circum-
stance that the presence of the most distinguished
liberals in Minster and the whole University
staff could confer.

The class-rooms at St. Mary's were numerous
and large ; there was in addition to them a well-
built house which had been occupied by Mr.
Lumley and his boarders.

The managers reserved this house; and, as a private speculation, furnished it for the reception of twenty girls, and appointed a certain Miss Flint as superintendent of what was known as *The House*.

For two years things went smoothly. The number of pupils in college and house increased steadily; the popularity of the founders was undiminished; they bore their honours meekly and well deserved the praise bestowed upon them.

Gratitude and courtesy combined to give them unlimited power both in the General Council, of which they had all been appointed members, and in the Ladies' Committee, where they formed a majority.

At the end of this period the health of Lady Mary Ellice, never very strong, failed entirely, and a lengthened residence in the south of Europe was prescribed for her. No greater catastrophe than that which was brought about by her absence could have befallen the council and committee of St. Mary's. She had given strength to the gentle and yielding Mrs. Milner, and supplied the want of words in Miss Julia Spiers. The friends of Miss Julia Spiers opined that she might think although she did not speak, and that it was not impossible she should form

opinions though she never uttered them. She
did in reality blindly follow the three managing
ladies. She looked up to them as her leaders
and voted for everything of which they approved.

Shortly after Lady Mary left Minster for
Cannes, Mrs. Armstrong received a letter signed
J. de S. Kimberley Finch, which she thought of
such importance that it was brought forward for
consideration at the ensuing meeting of the
Ladies' Committee. Miss Kimberley Finch stated
that she had followed the career of St. Mary's
with deep interest ; that the *Emancipation and
Advancement of Woman* was the only subject
deserving attention at the present time ; that if
the movement in their favour was not judiciously
guided, the advantages now offered would be
allowed to slip away from them, and the sole
result of all labour on their behalf would be to
increase the emoluments and add to the power
of men. She spoke with authority on this
matter, for she said her brother was a well-known
English professor in Dublin University, and she
appealed with confidence to the experience of
every woman to confirm her statements. They
were all familiar with the universal masculine
belief that women have nothing to do with their

money except to bestow it in some manner for the advantage of men. "As for men," she continued, "women are absolved from all consideration of their interests. They will look after themselves; they always have done so. They will snap up every penny that is to be had, and take the bread of knowledge from the very lips of women, though they are liberal enough with the cold water of disapproval. In almost every parish in England, at some period, money has been left for the education of boys and girls. What have the men done? On the plea of the inability of women to understand and manage business they have assumed entire control over it, and spent it on endowed schools and grammar-schools for boys. If they have occasionally reserved a trifle for girls, how has it been employed? A charity-school has been established in which a certain number of poor girls are dressed like scarecrows, treated like felons, taught to destroy crockery by having nothing but tin mugs and plates, and sent out into the world unable to write their names or to read the alphabet; ignorant, stupid, and vicious. In fact," concluded the writer, "the influence of men in an institution established for the benefit of Woman can have only one result; to maintain

their own supremacy and confirm the degradation of our sex."

When this letter was read some members of
the committee laughed and some protested;
but the managing ladies maintained a solemn
silence; they were considering the fact that
they had received no interest for their
money.

If Lady Mary had been present she would
have recognised the nature of this cloud on the
horizon, and have provided means to escape from
the danger which it threatened. But in her
absence no one had the requisite tact and the
necessary social influence to smooth over little
difficulties. Miss Ellen Green had been pro-
moted to the chair, and was supposed to take
Lady Mary's place. She was nervous and irritable, and chiefly troubled by Mrs. Brownlow, the
wife of one of the Professors, a young and very
pretty woman who chattered freely. It was
Mrs. Brownlow who now broke the silence of the
meeting by observing:

"I have heard of Professor Finch. I think
my husband knows him, and his sister is so
disagreeable that I believe he is obliged to make
extra-mural arrangements in order to procure his
meals in peace."

" Hush, Bell !" exclaimed a cousin who sat by Mrs. Brownlow's side.

Miss le Mesurier, turning to the two ladies, said harshly :

" No doubt a man is very glad to escape from his sister when he finds in her an intellectual equal."

" I should have expected it to be the other way :" exclaimed Mrs. Brownlow. " I am always sorry for a man who is tied to a disagreeable, nagging woman ; and a sister must be worse than a wife because you can't beat her."

Miss Ellen Green rapped the table sharply, and Mrs. Nichol appealed to her cousin. As a result that lady broke out into whispers, but made no further audible remarks throughout the meeting.

Mrs. Milner proposed that Miss Kimberley Finch should be thanked, and informed that St. Mary's had been established entirely through the generous interest and influence of Principal Ellice and the professors of Minster University ; but · Miss le Mesurier protested strongly that such a statement would be partial and misleading, and proposed that Miss Kimberley Finch should be asked for an opinion on the present condition of affairs.

And thus it was that Miss Kimberley Finch was thanked and encouraged. One letter was followed by another, and a policy of distrust and suspicion was inaugurated, which had begun to break up the harmony of the Ladies' Committee and of the General Council. The managing ladies hesitated to take any step without the advice of Miss Kimberley Finch, and appealed to her on every possible occasion.

Mrs. Armstrong and Miss le Mesurier were always ready to follow her advice and take the initiative in offensive measures; but Miss Ellen Green was a woman of a different stamp; narrow it is true, suspicious and irritable, a woman of weak nerves and weak health, but naturally susceptible to good influence, and not incapable of aspiration. Under a leader like Lady Mary Ellice she would have carried on her work to noble issues. Even now she had occasional accesses of compunction which troubled her colleagues and impeded their progress; but in spite of these they had, during the period that had elapsed since the receipt of the first letter from Miss Kimberley Finch, contrived to change the whole aspect of affairs at St. Mary's, and had obtained a position which enabled them to worry the professors, interfere in the teaching, suggest inspec-

tion, and urge external examinations. By degrees
during this period ready acquiescence in all their
views had given place to organised resistance on
the part of the professors; and this again was
met by persistent and determined attack on that
of the managers.

At length, after some years of discord, the
council accepted a suggestion emanating in the
first place from Miss Kimberley Finch, that a Lady
Resident should be appointed, and made responsible for the condition of the college. The Professors, groaning under many masters, had eagerly
adopted the suggestion. They declined, however,
to elect the candidate put forward by Miss Kimberley Finch, and preferred to wait for the result
of an advertisement to be inserted in *The Times*.

This advertisement was answered by two hundred and ninety-seven candidates, of whom two
hundred and twenty-five could not write a gram-
matical letter or spell it correctly. Of the re-
maining seventy-two only nine gave promise of
being competent, and this number was rapidly
diminished to two ; Miss Crayston and the candidate originally brought forward by Miss Kimberley Finch.

Miss Crayston, who held testimonials that were
unimpeachable, and who was known to belong to

a good family and believed to possess private means, was chosen by the Ladies' Committee and elected by the Council, chiefly, as the managers were well aware, on the ground that she was *not* their nominee.

It was the first severe check which the three ladies had received, and they looked upon it, so Miss le Mesurier said, as "a most unmerited insult."

"Perhaps you are wrong," urged Mrs. Armstrong. "I think from the photograph that she must be just the kind of person we want."

CHAPTER V.

THE short January afternoon is fast drawing to a close. The wind is rising. It whistles past the windows in angry gusts, driving before it low dark clouds. Whenever there is a lull wandering snowflakes are seen, or there is a sudden burst of sleet and hail. A dull, continuous reverberation seems to fill the air; from time to time it is interrupted by a sound like the boom of artillery.

The sea is nearly two miles distant; but in a storm on the Cornish coast, with a gale from the north-west, the long roll and mighty sweep of the Atlantic waves brings them thundering over the cruel reefs at the foot of the cliff with the crash and the tramp of armies.

The brunt of the storm falls upon the cliffs which shelter the Minster valley; but it is also felt

in the old city that lies on the steep south-
eastern slopes, and the ladies who brave such
inclement weather in order to reach St. Mary's
Hall have shown considerable courage. Not a
few of them, as they sit round the committee-
table, look from time to time anxiously towards
the windows. They think of the gathering storm
and the darkness; of the half-mile of exposed
road which separates them from the ruined tower,
the battered walls of a cathedral, the cluster of
halls, chapels, and old-fashioned houses, the low-
lying lanes and purlieus, the light and warmth
and dirt and noise, the human fellowship and
shelter of the old University and city of Minster.
They reflect, moreover, that only one of their
members has a carriage, and that she has never
been known to overcrowd it.

The nine ladies in St. Mary's Hall are seated
round a table covered with green baize. They
have pens, paper, and ink before them, and a
casual observer may at once discover that they
represent the product of the nineteenth century,
a Ladies' Committee. The institution over which
they preside is a Ladies' College. One of their
number is absorbed in a pen-and-ink sketch of
a young man followed by a dog, another ex-
ecutes a highly-finished drawing of an oak leaf,

and the remainder are talking together in little
groups of two and three.

There is an animated discussion on the tem-
perance question at one side of the table, whilst
on the other the announcement that Colonel
Black is to rejoin his regiment in India, and that
Mrs. Black will let Trelawney and go abroad
with the children, is received with great interest.

At the head of the table a large fair woman
in spectacles beams mildly and somewhat feebly
over the assembly.   By her side is the honorary
secretary, Mrs. Armstrong, who clears her throat
with a prolonged er—er—er—um, and tries in
vain to attract attention.   Mrs. Armstrong is
about fifty years old and a widow, at least she is
supposed to be a widow.   Mr. Armstrong, who
left her three years after their marriage to look
after some property in the colonies, has never
since either written or returned to her.   She does
not speak of him to anyone.   After he had been
absent twelve years she put on mourning, which
she has now worn for six years.   "I have every
reason to believe that my husband is dead," she
said to her friends; but she said no more, and
declined to answer questions "on so painful
a subject."   Mrs. Armstrong has very light hair,

so light that it is difficult to discriminate between the grey and the sandy, colourless eyes
with a gleam of pale blue when she is angry,
and a round face on which hair grows in tufts
and patches, chiefly on moles in the region of
the mouth and chin. Her teeth, which project,
are large, long, and set far apart. She draws
her lips over them when she is silent, and this
gives a look of repression which is her characteristic expression. She has before her a pile of
official-looking books and papers, and by her side
gapes a leather bag full of letters and miscellaneous documents. These letters used formerly
to be brought to the table in a simple but com-
modious wooden box, in which they were neatly
arranged. On one occasion the box was unfor-
tunately turned away from the owner and towards
the assembled members of the Committee. The
announcement on the inside of the lid, "Fry's
Homœopathic Cocoa, grateful, nourishing:" produced a general smile, and an after ripple of
laughter through the small Minster circle, which
did not fail to reach Mrs. Armstrong. She
thereupon abandoned the box and adopted a
bag with an ominous steel snap, and pockets
in which small documents were sure to be mislaid.

A loud gust of wind for a moment hushes all voices, and the speakers look uneasily towards the windows.

"I wish to remark," observes one of the members, "that it is now more than an hour since the Lady Resident ought to have arrived."

"Perhaps there has been an accident," interposes her neighbour. "Have you heard about poor Bessie Polwarth ?"

"Is she the one that went to visit her aunt at Sheffield ?"

"The very same ; Bessie. Well, when she reached Exeter she stepped out of the carriage too soon——"

"I beg your pardon," interrupts a harsh, discordant voice ; "she got out too late."

"I *think* you are wrong, Miss le Mesurier ; I had it from a friend who is sure to know, and she says——"

"I am sorry to interrupt the conversation," interposes Mrs. Armstrong; "but we have business of great importance before us."

"Is it about Miss Ravenshaw ?" asks Mrs. Nicholl.

"That matter was decided at our last meeting, when you were not present :" smiles Miss Ellen Green, who always likes to remind people of the non-fulfilment of their duties. "Miss Flint cannot at present receive another boarder, and Mr. Ravenshaw made rather a point of placing his daughter under Miss Crayston's charge. We have acceded to his wish, and in so doing have secured a companion for Miss Crayston, a pupil for the college, and a very desirable connection."

"Hear, hear!" exclaims Miss le Mesurier.

"Did you not say," asks Mrs. Brownlow, "that when the minutes were read and confirmed we should have nothing to do except to receive the Lady Resident?"

"I don't think those words were used," replies Mrs. Armstrong, smiling at Miss Ellen Green and speaking for her, "at the same time I was not aware until this morning of the important matters I should have to bring before you."

"Can't you postpone the communication?"

"I think not. The fact is, I have received a long letter from Miss Kimberley Finch, which contains most valuable advice as to the position and duties of the Lady Resident."

"But we decided those points at our last meeting!"

"You see," resumes Mrs. Armstrong, "that Miss Kimberley Finch has had so much experience, and is such a very distinguished authority, that I am sure we shall all be disposed to modify our decisions if they are such as she does not approve."

Mrs. Armstrong looked round the table; the lady in the chair bowed graciously, and Miss le Mesurier nodded her head with a jerk.

" Will it not be a very good plan to send the letter round from one member to another ? " asked Mrs. Cookson, laying down her pen, and contemplating the oak-leaf with some satisfaction.

" It would be a great loss of time, and scarcely courteous to Miss Kimberley Finch, who has taken the trouble to write expressly for this meeting."

" I shall be delighted to propose a vote of thanks to Miss Finch : " interposed Mrs. Brownlow with alacrity; " and I suggest that the letter shall be entered upon the minutes."

" No, no," whispered her neighbour; " we shall then have it twice over."

" Shall we ? Oh ! then, if you please, Mrs. Armstrong, I don't propose it."

" We can scarcely impose such a task upon our secretary as to transcribe *all* the letters that are received, however important they may be : " said Miss Ellen Green, the lady in the chair. She smiled at Mrs. Brownlow as one conscious of superior knowledge with regard to the details of committee work ; and this smile, which was her strong point, often did more than words to over-awe her colleagues.

As no one replied, she continued :

"Moreover, we have not yet decided whether this letter is or is not important, so I will ask Mrs. Armstrong to read it."

Mrs. Brownlow and her cousin and inseparable companion, Mrs. Nicholl, always sat together at the Committee meetings, and carried on much private conversation.   As the result of an em-phatic whispered appeal Mrs. Nicholl now said :

" May I delay the reading for a few minutes to ask how it is that when we had decided to give the new porter and his wife £60 a year they have been engaged at £40 ? "

" I don't think we can re-open the question:" smiled Miss Green.

" The minutes confirming the appointment at £40 a year were signed at our last meeting, Mrs. Nicholl, which you did not attend:" said Mrs. Armstrong.

" Yes ; but I find that no one noticed the change from £60 to £40, and we are all quite sure that we voted the former sum, although Miss le Mesurier proposed the latter."

"The porter is already complaining of his poor pay, and no wonder : " said Mrs. Brownlow.

"I don't see that there is anything to be done :" said Miss Green, looking at Miss le Mesurier, who shook her head.

"My husband suggests that we had better have the minutes rectified, or something of that kind," continued Mrs. Nicholl; "the gentlemen will tell us how to manage it."

"Ah," smiled Miss Ellen Green, "Professor Nicholl is not very familiar with the business of a LADIES' Committee ; but perhaps Mrs. Armstrong will kindly explain."

Thus appealed to, that lady turned over the contents of the leather bag, and produced a bulky document. She retained it in her hand whilst she announced that, as the decision with regard to the porter's salary was in direct opposition to the advice given on that subject by the managing ladies, she had thought it better to consult Miss Kimberley Finch. That lady, who had great experience in all these matters, considered that £60 a year would be full London wages for a man and his wife, and would be excessive at St. Mary's. The managers, acting upon this advice, had therefore decided in favour of the sum originally proposed.

"Now, really!" exclaimed Mrs. Brownlow. "How nice for you! And that was exactly your own opinion, Mrs. Armstrong! Was it not?"

"I anticipated your objections," replied Mrs. Armstrong, with some asperity, "and therefore wrote again to Miss Kimberley Finch on the subject. She states that the secretary of a committee has very large discretionary powers, and she does not see that I have in any way exceeded them. I will read what she says on the subject:" and she opened the voluminous document and began to read.

There was a feeble attempt on the part of two or three members to put further questions; but Mrs. Armstrong read on and on, stumbling over words, and correcting herself so often that it was not easy to gather her meaning. This manner of reading was habitual to her; and Mrs. Brownlow, in a whisper to her cousin, who complained that she could make nothing of it, replied:

"Depend on it there's method in her madness."

The letter seemed interminable; but when it passed from the discussion of the porter's salary to the appointment of visitors to the classes, and the exclusion of the wives of the Professors from the class rooms, the whole committee was roused to attention.

"This, my love," whispered Mrs. Brownlow,

"this is the use of rockets, so valuable in savage warfare."

"Hush, don't be foolish. It is no time for jesting."

"Am I to understand," asked a lady who had not yet spoken, "that a decision has been formed, and a new scheme inaugurated, of which this committee is ignorant?"

Mrs. Armstrong hesitated.

"Well, really, Miss Graham, as the founders are members of the committee, and form a majority, we cannot be said to be ignorant even in our corporate capacity."

"I'll make a note of 'corporate capacity:'" murmured Mrs. Brownlow, as she drew pen and paper towards her.

"But is the decision of the founders binding upon the committee?"

"Most assuredly:" replied Miss Ellen Green with a smile of ineffable condescension.

"How delightful for the founders!" exclaimed Mrs. Brownlow, this time aloud; and she looked so simple, so young, and so pretty, that Miss Ellen Green was beguiled, and added, with much affability:

"But you forget the grave responsibility of their position, dear Mrs. Brownlow."

"Perhaps I do:" replied that lady, with an artless and beaming look, which quite re-assured Miss Ellen Green. "Perhaps I do:" she added, as if thinking aloud; "and it would be only kind of you to tell us some of their other secret decisions before we come upon them head-foremost in the letters of Miss Kimberley Finch."

Mrs. Armstrong moved uneasily upon her chair, and Miss Green coloured:

"We have been compelled to take the step now announced:" she said, "and before long the whole committee will see the necessity for, as well as the wisdom of it."

The rasping voice of Miss le Mesurier was now heard.

"We know what men are:" she said, "they like supreme power, and always contrive to get it; now we *must* keep the government of the College in our own hands. Besides, our numbers are increasing, and there will soon be a great many young girls about the place; we must have strict rules, and must be able to remonstrate with the Professors if necessary."

"I am not quite sure that I understand you:" urged Mrs. Brownlow, turning a beaming face upon the severe visage of the last speaker, who

was at the far end of the table ; " but I am quite
sure that if ever my husband flirts with any of
the young ladies, or the old ones either, I should
like to remonstrate with him myself."

"This subject should not be treated with
levity :" interposed Mrs. Armstrong, and three or
four ladies who had laughed looked uncomfortable at her reproof.

"That is my view :" said Mrs. Nicholl, coming
to the relief of her cousin. " If the Professors
are to be treated like schoolboys, watched and
worried——"

"I might as well inform you, as a fact,"
interrupted Mrs. Armstrong, " that the original
promoters of the College have, by the advice of
Miss Kimberley Finch, already come to a decision
on this point. We held a meeting a week ago,
and our conclusion was *unanimous*."

"Not unanimous :" said a low, sweet voice,
" Lady Mary was not present, and I opposed the
measure. I think it most inexpedient, most unjust, and most discourteous towards the gentlemen
upon whose generous assistance we depend for
the success of our scheme."

Miss le Mesurier, red and angry, had in vain
attempted to interrupt the speaker.

"Really, Mrs. Milner, I must protest against

such a breach of confidence as the repetition of what took place at a founders' meeting."

"Let us have a dictionary :" suggested Mrs. Brownlow, "and look out the meaning of *unanimous*. One does forget one's long words."

Mrs. Armstrong kept back an angry rejoinder with some difficulty, and after a moment's pause turned to Mrs. Milner saying :

"I consulted Miss Kimberley Finch on this very point, and she assures me that, considering the strength of our convictions and the importance of our cause, we are fully justified in considering the decision *unanimous*."

Mrs. Armstrong closed her mouth with an ominous snap and drew down the lips over her large teeth.

Mrs. Milner sighed, Mrs. Brownlow and Mrs. Nicholl whispered to each other, and then there was silence, broken a few minutes later by the harsh tones of Miss le Mesurier.

"The fact is," she said, "that the Professors and the ladies represent antagonistic interests. We care for nothing but the welfare of woman, and therefore we must take immediate steps to secure the entire management of the College."

By way of dropping oil upon the troubled waters this speech was about as successful as any

ordinary utterance of Miss le Mesurier. There
arose a murmur on all sides.

"I don't think that is *exactly* what we said :"
interposed Miss Ellen Green, "though the clear,
forcible statements of Miss le Mesurier are never
very far wrong," the two ladies smiled blandly
upon each other, "perhaps Mrs. Armstrong will
explain."

Thus appealed to, Mrs. Armstrong, who spoke
as she read, with hesitation, frequent correction,
and numerous pauses, proceeded to say :

"I must confess that we were all, nearly
every one of us, very much impressed by the
view Miss Kimberley Finch takes of our position.
She says that the existing Colleges for men are
so, in fact are what they are, because you see
they are governed by men ; and that if ever ladies'
colleges are to be the same, in fact what they
ought to be, they must be governed by women."

"That *so*," whispered Mrs. Brownlow, "is most
impressive."

"Oh, pray be quiet."

"I have good reason to believe," continued
Mrs. Armstrong, turning her eyes upon the
speaker with a reproving glance, in reply to
which Mrs. Brownlow smiled and nodded, "I
have in fact *evidence*, that the London Colleges

regret that they did not seize upon this as a vital principle. We have to show that the powers of women are, in fact, indeed that they are most certainly of a higher order than those of men; and so we ought to, in fact we *must*, secure all offices of trust, importance, and dignity connected with the College."

"The committee will remember," said Miss Graham, "that these are the views of a lady whom we have never seen, and of only a few of the ladies present. They do not certainly represent the unanimous opinion of the ladies' committee, nor are they shared by the general council, which consists of ladies and gentlemen——"

"Very unequally divided," angrily interrupted Miss le Mesurier.

"It never occurred to us that there was any *division* in the matter:" continued Miss Graham. "The general council has administrative and the ladies' committee executive functions."

"Oh dear, dear:" sighed Mrs. Brownlow.

"I think I must really be going home," said Mrs. Nicholl; "it is getting very late, and the subject now under discussion is one in which I am not competent to take any part."

"Pray do not leave us, Mrs. Nicholl:" said Mrs. Milner, in her low sweet tones; and then turning from one to the other, she urged all present to have patience, to wait until plans were further developed, to take no irrevocable step too soon (at this point Mrs. Armstrong replaced all her papers and closed the bag gently), and to try and secure the hearty co-operation of all those interested in the great work before them.

"I'll keep Jack up to his work :" murmured Mrs. Brownlow. "She is the very dearest old lady I ever knew."

Mrs. Milner continued speaking, and insensibly she drew her listeners away from the dangerous topic of the respective powers and merits of men and women to the advent of the new Lady Resident.

"I must confess," she said, taking up the photograph of an elderly and foreign-looking female, "I must confess to a shade of disappointment in the personal appearance of Miss Crayston. I had hoped from an indescribable something in her letters that she was young and," she added after a moment's pause, "good-looking."

"Oh, please tell me how you find that out from a letter :" eagerly asked Miss Julia Spiers, who had hitherto remained silent.

It was ruled from the chair that an explanation on this point was inadmissible; but Mrs. Milner's statement had been successful in diverting attention from all that preceded it. The disadvantages of youth and good looks were freely discussed, and were being demonstrated by Mrs. Armstrong on the authority of Miss Kimberley Finch, when Mrs. Brownlow, drawing out her watch, exclaimed:

"Do you know it is nearly five o'clock? We have been here since a quarter to three. Miss Crayston cannot be coming to-day, and I really must not wait any longer."

"It is now precisely three minutes *after* five:" said Mrs. Armstrong with emphasis, looking at a large silver watch which she drew from a breast pocket on the outside of a tight-fitting cloth jacket. "Is that your time, Miss Graham?"

"I am *seven* minutes after five:" replied that lady.

"You are both wrong:" said Miss le Mesurier in the tone of one who conveys a moral reproof; "it is exactly four minutes after five. My watch may be relied on."

"I wonder who came in that cab that drove to the door nearly an hour ago."

"I didn't see any cab."

F 2

"Yes, it came just after Gibson lighted the gas; I heard it distinctly."

"We had better ring and ask:" said Miss Graham, going to the bell.

"It will be perfectly useless to do so:" exclaimed Mrs. Armstrong. "My instructions to Gibson were quite clear. I said, 'Gibson, when Miss Crayston arrives you will usher her into the council chamber.'"

"Poor Gibson:" murmured Mrs. Brownlow; "perhaps he doesn't know how to usher."

In answer to the bell appeared a man with straight black hair, and a very white face deeply pitted by small-pox.

"You remember, Gibson," said Mrs. Armstrong, determined to show that she had prepared for the event of the day, "you remember what I desired you to do upon the arrival of Miss Crayston?"

"Yes, mum; Miss Crayston, mum, is '*ere.*"

"*Here!* pray what do you mean? *Where* is she?"

"She's in 'er own privit apartiament, mum, a takin' tea along of Professor Walmsley."

"Oh, my love!" ejaculated Mrs. Brownlow in a whisper, with a squeeze of her neighbour's hand.

There was profound silence, and the porter, looking round the table, added :

" She come about four o'clock.

No one spoke. Gibson waited a few moments and then left the room.

" This is a bad beginning!" groaned Mrs. Armstrong, " a very bad beginning."

Miss Ellen Green leant back in her chair and sighed deeply.

But Miss le Mesurier sniffed the air and arose, saying : " I will go and enquire into it."

CHAPTER VI.

THE FIRST INTRODUCTION.

PROFESSOR WALMSLEY had walked up to St. Mary's for a book. He was waiting in the hall whilst the porter searched for it, when a cab drove to the door, and a small lady dressed in deep mourning stepped from it.

She looked round with a part-shy, part-expectant air, and her eyes naturally fell upon the Professor. He concluded that it was the new Lady Resident, and watched her with some interest, for there was much speculation concerning her in the College circle. When he saw a slight pale person, with a wistful look in her eyes, he stepped forward, and said with some hesitation:

"I suppose you are Miss Crayston. We shall soon be better acquainted, for I teach mathematics in St. Mary's. The porter is just now up-stairs, and no one seems to be about, so pray let me take you to your sitting-room."

She thanked him and entered.

"You have a room at the back of the house," he said, leading her along a dark passage, "which was formerly assigned to the Professors, so I know the way.

"I am afraid you are very tired:" he continued, turning to the silent companion who had followed him into a small bare room.

"Yes:" she replied, "I am tired. I came from Cheltenham, and although the distance is not very great it is a tedious journey, and I have been all day in the train."

She grew paler as she spoke, and the Professor saw that she was trembling.

"At this stage," he thought, "a woman either cries or faints; I wonder which she will do, and what I shall do."

The difficulty was solved by the appearance of Gibson.

"Oh, Gibson; go to Mrs. Armstrong at once and say that Miss Crayston has arrived."

"The ladies is in a comity, sir, and they expects me to husher Miss Crayston whensoever she arrives."

"Oh, she can't go yet; and you'd better wait a little. Stay; just tell your wife to make some tea."

He was proud of this inspiration, and went up

to Miss Crayston, who had heard him perfectly well, saying in rather a loud tone :

" I have ordered some tea for you."

She was standing before the window, looking out ; and she said, " Thank you :" without turning her head.

" No doubt she is crying : " he thought, but a moment after she turned her head, and he saw no sign of tears.

The Professor had got himself into a difficulty, and did not know how to get out of it. He did not see how he was to leave Miss Crayston ; and she did not help him to go. He was a very shy man, and was constantly doing some of the un-naturally bold things of which shy men alone are capable. In the present case he drew a chair to the fire, sat down with his feet on the fender, and began to rub his hands.

He looked at Miss Crayston with bewilder-ment. She was a young woman, which he had not expected ; tastes differ, and people seldom agree as to good looks, but, to put it mildly, the face seemed to him a pleasant one.

He gazed into the fire. " There's a surprise in store for some of our friends : " he thought : and then he turned to Miss Crayston, who this time looked at him.

She had not appeared to notice the cocoa-nut matting on which Mrs. Armstrong had decided as a durable and suitable covering for the floor of her sitting-room ; nor the walls, which were great blank spaces of yellow distemper ; nor the three cane chairs at three and sixpence, and the rickety American arm-chair, which cost six shillings ; nor the little deal table with its red and blue cotton cover.

She did not notice any of these things, but stood looking out over a long stretch of sand and grass towards a gap in the high cliff, where there was a line of light and a gleam of colour upon a distant sea.

"I shall like this : " she said, as she turned and met his gaze.

" Yes : " answered the Professor, replying to her thought rather than her words. " That sight of the sea gives us an escape into the infinite. It makes amends for many of the small vexations of life."

She smiled, and turning from the window sat down in the American chair and began to unfasten her shawl.

Mr. Walmsley went to her side and took it from her. She gave him her shawl and bonnet, and, looking up, she thanked him. No doubt she was accustomed to receive attention. She was quite calm and unmoved. She did not even tell him where to put them, but looked towards the window and the sea. He stood by her side and watched her with a strange feeling of compunction. Now that the crape bonnet and heavy veil, which he did not know what to do with, had been removed, there could be no doubt about her beauty. Thick plaits of brown hair were wound round her head, and where the light touched them gleams of gold made him think of the crown of a queen. Colour was returning to her pale cheeks and lustre to her eyes, whilst, when she spoke or smiled, the parted lips of a resolute and yet sensitive mouth showed small and very pretty white teeth.

The Professor began to feel sorry for her. He was sure the managing ladies would not like her; and he wished something could be done to modify the effect of a first impression. So he said, in a puzzled kind of way :

" Won't you keep on your bonnet till you have seen the committee ? "

" Oh dear no : " she said, looking at him with some astonishment as he held it out towards her; " no, indeed, thank you. I have had it on long enough, and now you see I am at home."

" Oh, so you are. Well, I suppose that makes

a difference." And with some reluctance he put the bonnet on a chair, laid the shawl above it, and pressed it down; then he resumed his seat, and sat looking into the fire with his feet upon the fender. Getting away seemed more hopeless than ever, for Miss Crayston did not speak. He could not think of anything to say as an excuse for leaving her, and it did not occur to him that no excuse was wanted.

The tea was slow in coming, for the porter's wife was not prepared for such a demand, or for the fact that the Lady Resident would arrive after a long day's journey. Still it was not so much commissariat as administrative difficulties that troubled her, and had led to an argument with her husband.

"Don't you remember now," said the porter, "what she said? 'Mrs. Gibson,' says she, 'you'll wait on the Lady Resident.' Them was her very words, no later than last night, a-standing 'ere by the side of this table. Now was they or was they not?"

"Well, James, far be it from me to contradick you, or say anything contrairy; but did she or did she not say, as she was a-going out of this servants' 'all, and turned back and took 'old of the door, just where I am now, and as it might be like this, did she or did she not say : 'Gibson, you will convey letters, messages, parcels, in fact *everythink*, to the Professors ? "

" Them was her words, Mary, I grant."

" Well, and if Professor Walmsley ordered the tea, James, you may be sure he wanted a cup for hisself. Now who's to take it in ? If I go near the gentleman I shall have her ragin' mad at me ; and go I won't."

"But what's the good of shovin' it all on to me ; don't I get enough of it all day long ! Tea was ordered for Miss Crayston, and it's you as must take it to her."

Finally, and after much discussion, it was agreed that Gibson should open the door, and his wife should carry in the tray ; that he should arrange the tea-cups, and that they should leave the room together.

When at last they made their appearance Miss Crayston, leaning back in the American chair, looked so pale and tired that Mrs. Gibson, a kind-hearted little woman, forgot all pre-cautions. She poured out a cup of tea and took it to her, asking at the same time if there was anything she could do to oblige her.

" Nothing, thank you."

" Me and Gibson, miss, will take up your boxes."

"Thank you."

"Me and Gibson, miss, will be most 'appy to try and make you as comfable as we can."

"Thank you," this time with a smile; "I will ring presently and ask you to show me my room."

"Quite the lady:" said Mrs. Gibson to her husband when they had returned to the room dignified by the title of servants' hall, "it's easy to see that; and much more so, I should say, than many. Poor thing! I shouldn't like to stand in 'er shoes."

"There's that bell a-ringin'," exclaimed Gibson, "and there let it ring; I know which on 'em that is. When Miss le Mesurier's in the 'ouse 'er 'and is never hoff it."

"Lor, James, don't you know she lives in lodgin's and ain't got nobody to order about, for they won't stand it; but there, do go, or she'll be down-stairs prying about. I 'eard 'er come out-side the door as soon as ever she'd rung."

When Gibson appeared Miss le Mesurier was standing in the hall. On second thoughts she had come to the conclusion that it would be rather derogatory to fetch the Lady Resident. She resolved therefore to send a message by the porter, and return to the council chamber,

where she would await the arrival of the delinquent.

Gibson conveyed the summons to Miss
Crayston, who rose at once to obey it. Her
companion was more puzzled than ever as to
how he was to get away ; and therefore, to the
surprise of the committee, when Miss Crayston
appeared she was attended by Professor Walmsley. After she had entered the room he closed
the door cautiously, took out his handkerchief
and wiped his brow ; and then espying Mrs.
Brownlow and Mrs. Nicholl hurried to them and
shook hands eagerly, as if, instead of having
met that very morning, he had not seen them
for years.

This was aggravating. It disarranged all Mrs.
Armstrong's plans. She had a certain document
in her bag with which she had hoped to strike
an early and effective blow, but it would be impossible to make use of it whilst a Professor was
present. However, she looked towards the new-
comer, and, without rising from her chair, said
with peculiar emphasis :

" Good *evening*, Miss Crayston."

Mrs. Milner had risen, and moved slowly towards the new official. She took her by both
hands and looked earnestly at her, and with some

astonishment depicted on her countenance, as she spoke a few kindly words of welcome.

Mrs. Brownlow and Mrs. Nicholl broke away from the Professor and greeted her with much cordiality, whilst Miss Graham also rose to shake hands with her.

"How tired you must be!" said Mrs. Brownlow; "much too tired to attend to business, and there really is none of any importance. Now that we have had the pleasure of receiving you, I think the best thing we can do is to allow you a few days to rest and look about you."

"Ahem!" exclaimed Miss Ellen Green, rapping on the table with her knuckles, "I cannot quite agree with you, Mrs. Brownlow. The duties of our Lady Resident are so very onerous and important that it would not be right to allow her to pass a night in ignorance of them."

"Perhaps Professor Walmsley has been explaining them:" suggested Miss le Mesurier, speaking sharply.

"Impossible!" said Mrs. Armstrong. "The entire control over college officials and the arrangement of the details of their respective duties rests exclusively with the *ladies* of the committee."

"Ah! you see that you are an officer:" said

Mrs. Milner in her sweet, gracious manner; and
taking Miss Crayston by the hand she led her
forward to the light. That lady had been looking on in silence. She had a way of slightly
raising her brows, and fixing dark, luminous eyes
on a speaker, which was impressive, and just now
somewhat embarrassing. She looked from one
to the other, from those that welcomed to those
that smiled, as if they were pictures that puzzled
her.

"I *am* tired," she said, as she took her seat
at the table by Mrs. Milner, "but I can quite
well attend to business."

As she sat the light fell full upon her, and
all eyes were fixed upon her face. A door was
opened and hastily closed again. The Professor
had escaped.

"This is the most gorgeous joke I ever heard
of: " whispered Mrs. Brownlow. "I *am* glad that
we stayed, ain't you?"

"Hush! hush! what does it mean; has
Walmsley got a hand in it!"

Mrs. Milner's beautiful face, pale and clear, set
in snow-white hair, beamed with happiness as
she talked to her young companion. Whispers
passed from one lady to the other, and "Extraordinary!" "Requires some explanation!"

"Shameful!" were the exclamations that were heard.

Mrs. Armstrong was hurriedly throwing the papers out of her bag. She found what she required, and leaning forward said to Miss Crayston:

"May I ask whose photograph this is?" and she handed up the likeness of the severe female.

Miss Crayston received it calmly, but started with pleasure as she recognised it.

"Mine," she said, "my very own copy. How did you get it? It is the likeness of my dear friend and former governess, Fräulein Deiss, who is now dead. My name is on it. This *Helen Crayston* is in her own hand-writing. Nothing has grieved me more than the mysterious loss of this photograph. How did it come into your possession?"

"My dear young friend:" beamed Mrs. Milner, who could scarcely refrain from kissing the speaker, "we all thought it was a likeness of *you*, and you can't imagine how relieved I am at the mistake."

"But how has it come into the hands of the committee? The servant at my rooms in Cheltenham said a strange lady came one day and took it from the table, and nodded to her

and walked away. I could not imagine what
had become of it."

"Mrs. Armstrong produced it at a meeting of
the committee some weeks ago," said Mrs. Milner,
"and she will explain this delightful mystery."

Thus appealed to Mrs. Armstrong, in a cold
and angry tone and with much hesitation, proceeded to explain that the managers were naturally anxious to have some notion of the
personal appearance of the candidates for the
post of Lady Resident. They had been outvoted
at the General Council when they proposed to
ask for photographs. Miss Crayston's testimonials were so good that there could be no
doubt as to her fitness for the post of Resident if
she consented to undertake it, but none of them
had alluded to her age. The distance from Cheltenham precluded the possibility of a personal
interview, and therefore Mrs. Armstrong said she
had asked Miss Kimberley Finch, who happened
to be passing through Cheltenham, if she would
call and see the candidate, who was almost
certain to be elected. Miss Kimberley Finch
forwarded the photograph, and of course they
asked no further questions.

"Hurrah!" whispered Mrs. Brownlow, "I
thought she was in it."

Mrs. Armstrong hesitated so much, and seemed so uncomfortable, that Miss le Mesurier interposed :

"Perhaps," she said, "as this correspondence was carried on through me, I had better continue the narrative."

Mrs. Armstrong looked relieved, and Miss le Mesurier, whose harsh tones had startled even those who were accustomed to hear them, proceeded :

"Miss Kimberley Finch was on the point of leaving Cheltenham when she received my letter with the request to obtain Miss Crayston's photograph. She very kindly took the trouble to drive to that lady's lodgings, although they were in a most out-of-the-way part of the town. Miss Crayston was not at home, no one seemed to know anything about her movements, so Miss Kimberley Finch thought she had better go in and wait a little. Of course I *may* be mistaken, but, as I understand the account, it was the servant who produced this photograph; she must have known the circumstances under which Miss Kimberley Finch thought it well to receive it on behalf of the committee."

"The servant alluded to is a very truthful girl :" interposed Miss Crayston. "She has always told me that a strange lady took it from the table, and just nodded to her and walked away with it."

"I am quite sure," retorted Miss le Mesurier, "that Miss Kimberley Finch would leave an explanatory message; a dirty servant in a lodging-house is not to be relied upon."

Miss Ellen Green rapped upon the table and looked at Miss le Mesurier, who was silent.

"Some one stated at the committee that Miss Crayston was forty-eight:" exclaimed Mrs. Brownlow, with an amused look.

"We concluded from the photograph that she was over forty, and thought it unnecessary to enquire as to her exact age. The managers have always been anxious to secure the services of an experienced lady, and we judged from the photograph that we had secured such a person:" resumed Mrs. Armstrong, who spoke in an aggrieved tone.

"I am sure we all see that although we very much regret the misunderstanding as to the photograph, yet that it is impossible Miss Kimberley Finch can be in any way to blame. We must really exonerate her from all blame:" said Miss Ellen Green, looking round the table.

"Miss Crayston gazed earnestly first at one

speaker and then at another.   There was a pause, and she asked in a voice which secured attention by a certain ominous vibration :

" Is Miss Kimberley Finch present ? "

" Oh, no : " answered Mrs. Brownlow with eager delight ; " we have never beheld her in the flesh. She is an airy nothing to us : that is, she has got a long name, but no local habitation that I ever heard of."

" I beg your pardon ; she lives at Grittleton : " said Mrs. Armstrong.

There was no change in the tone in which Miss Crayston resumed :

" I must beg the lady who corresponds with her to inform her that in removing the photograph I consider she has taken a most unwarrantable liberty."

" And I must remind you," said Miss le Mesurier hotly, " that this is not at all a desirable attitude for you to assume towards the committee, which has exonerated Miss Kimberley Finch from blame."

" Really, Miss le Mesurier, I don't agree with you : " interposed Mrs. Brownlow.   " I don't know much about attitudes, but I am sure that if a stranger came into my house and took a photograph I should consider the act one of petty larceny; and so would you, Mrs. Milner, would you not?"

"You are impulsive, dear 'Mrs. Brownlow, and apt to say a little more than you mean. But Miss Crayston must see," and she turned to that lady, "that if we do not hold such strong views as our young friend, and are not prepared to sanction the expression 'petty larceny,' yet that we were ignorant of the manner in which the photograph had been obtained. I see how very much Mrs. Armstrong and Miss Ellen Green are annoyed, and I can't tell you how much I should be annoyed myself if the discovery of our mistake had not come in such a charming form:" and she laid her hand on that of Miss Crayston.

"Dear old lady," whispered the irrepressible member. "Isn't she gracious. Let us try and make it up, just to please her."

"Mrs. Armstrong," she said aloud, "I beg to withdraw the expression petty larceny; it came out on the spur of the moment, in fact it visited me unawares. I am sure Miss Finch meant well, and as it has turned out she has really done well."

"They would never have elected Miss Crayston if the managers had seen her:" she whispered to her cousin in explanation.

"It is too late for regret:" croaked Miss le

Mesurier; "but there has been a lamentable mistake."

"Indeed there has:" assented Mrs. Nicholl; "and how Miss Kimberley Finch could have taken the photograph without Miss Crayston's knowledge or consent I cannot imagine!"

"That is not my meaning."

"We are giving you a strange reception:" said Mrs. Milner to Miss Crayston; "and you look quite exhausted. I must beg to urge upon the committee that we adopt Mrs. Brownlow's suggestion, and adjourn for two or three days."

"If you have no further use for the photograph of Fräulein Deiss," said Miss Crayston, fixing her eyes on Mrs. Armstrong, "I shall be obliged if you will restore it to me."

"Well, I don't know:" replied that lady, closing the bag in which she had deposited it; "I don't know about that. You see the circumstances are rather peculiar, and seem to require some explanation. I should like to have it clearly shown that Miss Kimberley Finch obtained it in a justifiable manner."

"Quite so:" said Miss le Mesurier. "And how are we to know which lady we have elected? We certainly chose the original of the photograph."

"Oh, dear me!" interposed Mrs. Milner with a

bewildered look; "there surely can be no difficulty on that point. I understood Miss Crayston to say that her friend is no longer alive."

"That is not my meaning, Mrs. Milner :" said Mrs. Armstrong, "I hold this photograph in my private capacity and not as honorary secretary. Before I give it up in my official capacity I ought to have some proof of official possession."

"I can make that quite clear to you at any rate :" exclaimed Mrs. Brownlow, "for I saw you put it in your bag two minutes ago."

There was an angry flush on Mrs. Armstrong's face, and Miss Ellen Green interposed on her behalf :

"I think, Mrs. Brownlow, that we must all sympathise with Mrs. Armstrong's conscientious scruples. I learn these details with regard to the photograph for the first time, and so does she. We both regret the incident ;" and she turned to Mrs. Armstrong, who reddened and bowed. "It will be better, therefore, to reserve documentary evidence for further enquiry."

This utterance from the chair, which seemed to please the speaker, was not received with general approbation, and Mrs. Milner looked from one to the other as if to implore peace. She cast an appealing glance upon Miss Crayston, but that lady's very steadfast eyes showed no sign of relenting.

"She'll fight:" whispered Mrs. Brownlow, clapping her hands gently under the table. "She'll fight: and she'll have it out of that bag."

And so she did: and the committee broke up.

Mrs. Milner offered Mrs. Brownlow and Mrs. Nicholl seats in her carriage. As they were driving home she sighed deeply.

"It was indiscreet," she said, "most indiscreet. It would have been much better to leave the matter in our hands. She has made at least three enemies on the very first day of her arrival; and she is so young, so charming, just my ideal of what she ought to be in all other respects."

"Never mind, we will soon make it all right."

"Ah, my love, things are not easily made 'all right' in this world."

Meanwhile Miss Ellen Green, Mrs. Armstrong, and Miss le Mesurier, who had remained after their colleagues left the room, were standing round the fire.

They were mortified as well as annoyed. The restoration of the photograph, which had been insisted upon in spite of their opposition, implied blame.

"It is equal to a vote of censure," sobbed Miss

Ellen Green ; "and yet not one of us knew anything about it."

Naturally, at this point there was some recrimination : each lady thought the other might have said or done something that would have brought about explanation. They censured the absent friend, and finally discovered that the person really to blame was the Lady Resident. She had deceived them as to her age, her appearance, and, most probably, as to her acquirements.

"It's a regular hoax !" exclaimed Miss le Mesurier; " a regular hoax; and so we shall find by experience !"

"Do you think Walmsley is in it ? " asked Mrs. Armstrong.

" Well, he always wanted her to come, and was here to receive her. Don't you remember how he laughed when he looked at the photograph ? " replied Miss Ellen Green.

" Don't tell me !" ejaculated Miss le Mesurier. "It's a *planned thing*. We have fallen into a regular *trap*."

" After all she is but one," the ladies said, and smiled at each other, and were reconciled.

CHAPTER VII.

MRS. BROWNLOW AT HOME.

"Oh, Jack," exclaimed Mrs. Brownlow, as she burst into a tiny drawing-room, and threw her arms round her husband's neck, "I thought I should never live to get home, and tell you all that has taken place at the committee."

"I began to have my own fears on the subject, and should have been really anxious if I had heard Mrs. Milner's carriage pass. So long as I knew that she was at St. Mary's I thought there was hope for you."

"She brought us both home, Mary and me. And do you know, Jack, that she kissed me when she said good-bye."

"Her kiss must be a benediction."

"It really is; and do you know, Johnnie, it made the tears start to my eyes. I am sure I don't know why, though. Can you tell me? And although she did not say a word I felt so sorry for being foolish, and talking so much at the meetings. I am resolved not to sit by the side of Mary. I'll go and sit by Miss le Mesurier, and then I shall learn not to whisper all the nonsense that comes into my head."

" A very good resolution if you can only keep it. But what has kept you so late ? "

" Oh, the most supreme goings on ! John, I can hardly keep my senses when I think of it. Why, the old lady in the photo; with her hair dragged back, isn't Miss Crayston at all ! Our new Lady Resident is a most lovely young creature. As for Walmsley, I shall think worse of him than I ever did if he has an atom of heart left. He spent a whole hour with her, Jack, alone ! Why or how I can't imagine ; but I am sure the three think it was an assignation ; and as for them, Johnnie, they really are too cross and unhappy. Somehow I am a little sorry for them. See ! She stands and looks at you like this."

Mrs. Brownlow had thrown aside her hat and warm jacket as she was speaking ; and now she drew out comb and hair-pins, and wound a long coil of bright shining curls round her head, which strayed and fell in charming confusion.

" Now isn't that fine ? " she said.

" Very pretty indeed, my love, for a Bacchante."

" A Bacchante ! Why, she is Venus and Minerva combined."

" I don't like two-headed combinations, and I propose that we go to dinner."

" You are too much engrossed by material cares and pleasures, my husband. I tell you that this lovely lady is going to *live* here. She'll be in Minster, and one of us. I have made up my mind to have Shakespeare readings, and she shall have all the best parts. I was thinking it over on the way home, whilst Mary and Mrs. Milner were talking. We will begin with *Pericles*, and she shall take Marina."

" No, my dear; we will, if you please, begin with dinner."

" Nothing of the kind, Jack. You positively must listen to me. But don't be so greedy, and you may ring for dinner. I had forgotten those proofs ; and no doubt instead of correcting them this afternoon you have been reading the *Times*."

" And waiting for your return."

" Well, you will let me write for you after dinner, won't you ? and we'll have the boy and a real cosy evening."

" It sounds very delightful."

" Very well, then ; if it does, say that you are pleased about Pericles."

" My dear child, you may not be aware of it, but you have chosen the most difficult of Shakespeare's plays ; in fact, almost an impossible one for reading aloud."

" Details, my husband, mere details. Of course the parts will be marked. Now, if there is one thing that you have tried to impress upon me as the distinguishing mark of a mean mind it is absorption in details."

Mr. Brownlow laughed, and said,

"Quite true ; but these are details that give tone and colour to the play."

"Not so. Stop a minute and listen to me ; for I really do know what I mean this time. That young person, Marina, I mean, is set in the midst of the most tremendous evils, everything seems to be against her, bad men and worse women surround her, and you wonder what these swine will do with this pearl. She comes triumphant out of every danger ; and if I could only talk to you, John, as I ought to do, I would show you how Marina's purity does discover the purity that is hidden even in the people who seem so wicked. And then she doesn't preach and

argue. That's what I like. She looks up with
her angel eyes and says :

> 'Oh, that the gods
> Would set me free from this unhallow'd place,
> Though they did change me to the meanest bird
> That flies i' the purer air !'

That's quite enough. You know quite well
that she will come victorious out of every difficulty. And that is Miss Crayston. I see her in
a triumphal car and on a throne—"

"No, my dear ; what you really see is Anne,
announcing that dinner is on the table. Take
my arm."

"I don't know that I will. You ought to have
heard me to the end."

"So I will over the nuts and oranges ; and I
think you said something about the boy."

"Ah, that is where your heart is ; come along,
and we will take him with us."

They went to an adjacent room, where in his
little cradle a baby of eight months old was
lying with wide-open eyes. The mother sent
away a small maid who was sewing at a table
near the fire, and lifting her boy kissed him
repeatedly.

"Oh, John, look at him. Isn't he lovely ? His

cheeks and his little hands, the way his head is set, his sunny curls, and the nape of his neck, and then his little shoulders!"

The baby fixed steadfast eyes upon his mother and cooed to her as she spoke. She wrapped him in a soft white shawl and put him back in the cradle.

"Now, John, he is quite safe from the draughts of the passage, and you may carry the cradle down to the dining-room. We will put him on the hearthrug, and have him with us all the evening. And that is what a husband gets who is good to his wife and doesn't scold her when she is an hour late for dinner, and then detains him by her chattering."

"My dear, you mustn't put a premium upon your misdeeds."

"Be careful, John, or you'll say something about discounting my faults, and then you'll laugh so that you'll drop the cradle."

"Very good. I'll be guided by you."

"Shall I draw the bolt on our side of the door?"

"I think not; I have some work that must be finished, and I know that Nicholl is busy to-night. We had better wait a little."

Mrs. Brownlow had paused with her hand on

the bolt of a door at the foot of the staircase; a door of entrance into the adjacent house, occupied by the Professor of History, whose wife, Mary Nicholl, was Mrs. Brownlow's cousin and her senior by some eight years. In spite of this difference of age the cousins had always been fast friends. It was during one of her frequent visits to Mrs. Nicholl that pretty Isabel Evans met Mr. Brownlow, who was a well-known scholar at Oxford. When Isabel consented to be his wife he offered himself as a candidate for the vacant Professorship of Greek at Minster University. He was elected; and it was then that Mr. Nicholl secured for him the house next his own, and the friends resolved to open a door of communication in the wall that separated them.

"Mary," said the young wife when she took possession of her home, "I am delighted with the door; but I think there should be a bolt on each side of it."

"Oh, no; that is quite unnecessary. It will be enough to keep it always shut."

"It may be enough for you, but not for me. If I can get through that door I shall always be on the wrong side of it, looking after you and the babies. No, my love, it shall not be left open. We will have each a bolt, and you shall promise me not to unfasten that on your side of the house until dinner is over; and then we can spend our evenings together."

"Such nonsense!" replied Mrs. Nicholl. "Suppose some one is ill, or there is important news, or I want you."

"Oh, on great emergencies our rule does not hold good. But half the pleasure of living here will be gone if I can't pay you calls; in the morning if I want to see you I shall put on my hat and knock at the front door, and you can do the same."

Both the husbands approved of the suggested bolts, which, accordingly, were put on. The click of the withdrawal of the bolt was a signal that friends were welcome; but on this night the Brownlows did not as usual give the signal when dinner was over. Instead of that the cloth was hastily removed, Mr. Brownlow gave some letters to his wife, and instructed her as to the answers, and taking a packet of proof-sheets seated himself on the opposite side of the table. They worked in silence: Mrs. Brownlow wrote and addressed her letters, leaving them open that her husband might at his leisure see, as she said, if she had done her work properly. She

then rose, took a low chair to the side of her
baby's little cradle on the hearth-rug, and sat
down with her needlework. The boy was asleep.
His dimpled hand had firm hold of the corner
of a blanket, without which he could not go
to sleep happily. The mother kissed the little
hand, gently drew away the blanket, and arranged the cradle and her own seat so that her
husband could see his wife and child when he
raised his eyes from his work.

She knew that he liked to have them so in
his sight, with the fire-light shining upon her
whilst the darling face of his child, rosy and
pure, was seen under the shadow of the cradle
hood.

It was nearly ten o'clock when, after watching
her for some time unnoticed, Mr. Brownlow
said :

"My dear!" He never addressed her by
name; a husband who is twenty years older
than his wife very seldom does : "My dear!
why are you looking at the wall ?"

"I am planning the book-cases, Jack. I have
made up my mind to have them black, but with
lines of gold somewhere; I think at the very
top, or else I see that it won't do well with the
bindings of the books. And then we might

make a Landseer paper in grey-green do until we can afford paint, and panels, and that sort of thing."

"Perhaps you will kindly explain your meaning, my dear:" said the Professor, looking at the blotchy paper on the bare walls, the boxes of books piled one above the other, and the litter of magazines and newspapers in all parts of the room.

"Well, John, I have quite made up my mind that you must have book-shelves. Just think of the time you spend among those boxes, though you said they would be so convenient on the floor; and you know that the books you want are always out of the way! Now I have made up my mind that the back parlour shall be nursery and dining-room combined. I am not going to let this child turn out his father; and I shall make a real study for you, John; and won't you be proud!"

"I like the notion hugely; and some ten years hence we may be able to carry it out."

"You think so; well, look here:" and she approached and spread out before him a twenty-pound note. "There! My dear old mother has been saving and saving, ever since we were married, to send me this. She hoped to have got it by New Year's day, but it is a little late, because she had to wait for some dividends or something. Now I'll give it to you, John, if we really want it for the house ; but I'd like best to have it for my very own."

He looked at her with a sudden dimness that veiled his eyes, and then he laid his hand gently on the hand of his wife, which rested on the table, and there was a silence.

" John, I shall cry if you don't say something to me. I never had so much money before ; and I have kept the secret ever since one o'clock because I wanted to go to the Post Office and get the money. It did not seem possible that I should really have it ; and then I waited for this quiet time to tell you about it, our happiest time, dear Jack."

Her husband's voice was rather husky ; and he cleared his throat several times before he said :

" There are so many things that you want and the boy wants. I know the pleasure of giving ; but won't you get something with your money ? "

" I should think I would. I'll get more pleasure out of it than twenty pounds ever gave before. No man ever took such an empty-handed wife as you did, John."

"Rich with blessing and delight:" he said, as he stooped and kissed th ehand.

"I like that," she said; "do it again, John:" and then they both laughed, and in some mysterious way they had understood each other, and had no need to say any more about the money.

"You have been very good, and worked quite long enough; and you may carry the boy up-stairs. After that Mary and Mr. Nicholl shall come in just for half an hour."

"Very good, my dear:" and the Professor took up the cradle and carried it carefully up-stairs, followed by his young wife. They knelt together by the side of their boy, kissed him and covered the little hands, and left him sleeping peacefully. Never was baby so quiet, so good, they both agreed; and that wonderful gift of sleep which he had inherited from his mother was a natural endowment of greater value than a fortune, added the father.

When they returned to the dining-room Mr. Brownlow drew the bolt of the door of communication and called out:

"Nicholl, my wife has come into a fortune. Can you join us for half an hour, or is it too late?"

"Ah!" said his friend, a few moments afterwards, as he entered and saw the table. "You have been at work. Do you want those proofs posted to-night? If so I can take them with my letters."

"No, I have not finished; but I have done enough for to-day. The rest may wait, and I shall send all off together by the evening mail to-morrow."

The two men were soon engrossed in a discussion as to the meaning of a difficult passage.

"I will not allow it:" said Mrs. Brownlow, drawing a chair to the table; "and if there is one thing more than another that shocks my whole nature it is the profound dissimulation of which men are capable?"

"What do you mean?" asked Mr. Nicholl, who was always a little puzzled by his wife's cousin.

"Well, to hear you talk one would think you were discussing the driest and most learned book in the world, quite out of the reach of the average female intellect. Instead of which, Mary, I assure you," and she turned to Mrs. Nicholl, "this is a most jovial work. The manner in which you are told about the religious festival, and the people going from all parts to see it, and the servant that runs after a group of friends and takes one by the cloak and asks him to wait till

his master comes up, is just as simple as ever it
can be.   And then they all go home to supper
together, and there is a most delightful old man
in the chimney-corner.   He takes really a comprehensive view of things, and acknowledges
with the greatest candour that on the whole it is
better to be rich when you are old than to be
poor.   Just the conclusion my unenlightened
judgment would have led me to form ; so you see
how very superior I must be.   After that they
drift into an argument which is too deep for the
old gentleman ; he rises, and says it is time
for him to attend the religious ceremonies.   That
is the cleverest thing I ever heard, and I don't
intend to forget that old gentleman the next time
John is too many for me."

The men laughed, and Mr. Nicholl said :

" I am very glad to find, Mrs. Brownlow, that
you take so kindly to your Plato."

"Not at all," she said ; " it is not that.   The
thing I can't understand is the way in which you
all seem to forget what the books are about.   You
do nothing but talk about participles and things ;
and roots, and such like dry stuff ; editions, and all
that."

" My dear, your want of reverence is a painful

"John, it will be the making of you. You would grow dreadfully uninteresting with a woman that adored you. Now wouldn't he, Mary?"

"Perhaps; but let us talk over the fortune."

"No, no; not to-night. I want to gloat over it in secret and in silence."

"Very well; then we'll talk about something else. Have you told Mr. Brownlow all the Crayston episode?"

"No! I just began upon him before dinner; but I saw he was thinking about his proofs, so I waited for you. How I wish they could have seen Miss Crayston enter the room! Walmsley was there. He lost his hat and dropped his gloves, and went down on his hands and knees to find them. Then when we sat down he made a dart and disappeared."

"But what had he to do with the new Lady Resident?"

"That's the question, Mr. Brownlow; and if I am not mistaken it will be a burning one," replied Mrs. Nicholl.

"Jack, I shall never forget it:" exclaimed Mrs. Brownlow. "There had been breezes, or rather, as I have no doubt Professor Nicholl would like me to say, the vigorous initiative of the managing ladies had not been accompanied by ordinary courtesy."

"Don't consider me:" said the Professor laughing; "take your own way."

"My own way indeed! I tell you candidly that there is a new departure in our relations with the managers; but you shall hear."

"Perhaps, my dear, you will be more comfortable off the stilts."

"Thank you, John; I shall. Well, then, I shelved two or three letters from that dreadful woman in London. Now didn't I, Mary? Don't you let them laugh at me."

"Not altogether; but go on."

"We were all cross and a little tired, the gas was burning low——"

"When you heard three raps on a pane of glass."

"Not at all; and you must not interrupt me. I was thinking of my boy, and of what a shame it is to neglect him, and wondering how Mary and I could possibly get home through the storm if Mrs. Milner did not take us with her, when the door opened and in came, not a lady, but the Professor of History. He had his handkerchief in his hand, and he wiped his brow and looked at us in such an utterly be-

wildered manner that I really thought I must
have laughed. And then I spied a little black
thing far away in the gloom of that big room
near the door. Some of us went and shook
hands. I thought she was nice, for she has got a
skin like velvet, and the dearest little hand you
ever touched."

"My love, these are details that you may pass
lightly over, and spare our feelings."

"Be quiet, John. Well, when she came to
the light it was, I assure you, the most splendid
thing you ever saw. Her colour went and came,
her lips trembled just a little, and great solemn
dark eyes seemed to grow fuller and fuller of
light. I do assure you, John, I nearly went on
my knees to her. I really thought I should
cry."

"You must have recovered very quickly:" said
Mrs. Nicholl, "for when we sat down you poked
me and said: Beauty and the Beast. I haven't
the least idea what you meant."

"Pray don't ask me. Mr. Nicholl, the ladies
have appointed some one to look after you."

"What? some one else! Well, then, I hope
it is the Lady Resident."

"No, it is not."

"I have no doubt it is the lady who reproved

Mr. Walmsley for walking home with Miss Graham:" suggested Mr. Brownlow.

"That man is always getting into trouble!" was exclaimed amidst a general laugh. "What has he been doing?"

"You must ask my wife."

"Don't you know," resumed Mrs. Brownlow, "that after the last Council Meeting he walked home with Miss Graham? Miss Flint was shocked. She considered it a terrible example for the girls under her care in the boarding-house. Miss Armstrong said something about a vote of censure; and I believe Miss Kimberley Finch suggested a resolution and a sub-committee to regulate the intercourse of the Professors and the lady visitors. Ultimately Miss Ellen Green remonstrated privately with the offender, and he rushed off to Exeter by the next train."

"My dear, my dear, don't go too far!"

"It is impossible to go too far with regard to those ladies:" interposed Mr. Nicholl with some warmth. "They threaten to make life unendurable."

"Really, James:" said his wife laughing, "you are not free from blame. I have remonstrated with you over and over again on your unpunctuality."

"Now, Brownlow, I appeal to you. Whenever I go to St. Mary's I find Mrs. Armstrong standing at the foot of the staircase with a large silver watch in her hand. And each time that I pass she clears her throat and ostentatiously consults it."

There was a merry peal of laughter at his expense.

"My dear fellow, you should get there before her. We see her pass this window. She goes up on purpose for your class."

"That's what I tell him:" said his wife. "He might easily take his revenge, and leave her at the foot of the stairs for an hour."

"What fun!" exclaims Mrs. Brownlow. "Down comes the distinguished Professor, and as he passes Mrs. Armstrong he takes out *his* watch, clears his throat, looks at her, bows and walks away."

An indescribable, slight gesture suggested Mr. Nicholl's look and manner. After the laughter to which it gave rise had subsided Mr. Brownlow asked:

"Who is Miss Crayston? Didn't we hear something about her?"

"You must ask Mary," replied his wife; "she is up in her county families. She has got connections, John, on the father's side. Our mothers were sisters; but we haven't even a lawyer's clerk on my side of the house, as you know. Mary, naturally, always has taken an interest in the aristocracy."

"Miss Crayston," said Mrs. Nicholl calmly, "is one of the Craystons of Crayston Warren. So much we know from her reference to the family solicitor at Silchester; but not her exact position in the family. The head of it is Sir Lionel Crayston, a man of thirty-two years old, unmarried, and greatly impoverished by the extravagance of his father, Sir Hubert, who died three years ago."

"Ah, Mary, I remember the thrill of emotion with which some of our colleagues heard you give this information concerning Sir Lionel at the committee-meeting."

"Bell, I am ashamed of you. You know the subject was not even alluded to."

"Wasn't it, dear? Then I can imagine the thrill of emotion which would shake those tender——."

"Hush, hush! You're a silly monkey."

"Miss Crayston will be lonely at St. Mary's:" suggested Mr. Nicholl.

"Don't you remember that she asked permission from the council, two months ago, to have a

young lady to board with her and attend the
College classes?" said Mrs. Brownlow.

"Was it granted?"

"Yes; and I heard her telling Mrs. Milner just
before we left this evening that Miss Ravenshaw
is coming to her to-morrow. By the way, Mary,
who are the Ravenshaws?"

"I think this girl must be the daughter of
John Ravenshaw. He sold his estate in Wilt-
shire and settled near Westhampton. He has
had a great deal to do with ships, and has made
a very large fortune, or rather has very largely
increased his own, which was always considerable."

"Why did he sell his land?" asked Mr.
Brownlow.

"I am told that he married some one beneath
him. No one would visit her at first. He did
not act very judiciously; but just gave up his old
home and went to Westhampton."

"Is she a vulgar woman?"

"Not at all, I believe; an excellent mother
with an enormous family; a great, happy, healthy
household, which she keeps in good order without too great severity or undue license. I know
them through the Wilkinsons; and in fact
it is through me, indirectly, that Bertie, the

fourth daughter, is coming to Miss Crayston. I hear she is very clever and anxious to study; and just when I had been told this we were in the midst of arrangements regarding the new Lady Resident, so I suggested Miss Crayston to the Ravenshaws, through Miss Wilkinson, and they are to place their daughter with her."

Mrs. Brownlow looked at her cousin and sighed.

" You see, John," she said, " what it is to have· a wife who knows her county families. But, Mary dear, I am your own first cousin on the mother's side, and when you ask these two dis- tinguished young persons to afternoon tea, you'll let me sit in a corner and look on, won't you ?"

CHAPTER VIII.

WOMAN'S FUTURE.

IT was six weeks since Bertie had left home, and she was sitting among the students in the lecture-hall of St. Mary's College for Women.

A short, square-shouldered man stood before a wooden desk which was placed on a small raised platform at one end of a large and lofty hall. He stooped over a manuscript from which he was reading; and from time to time raised his head to throw back the long dark hair that grew low on his brow and fell before his eyes whenever he held down his head. It was in vain that he shook it back or thrust his hand through it.

" 'Tis against nature : " murmured Mrs. Brownlow, who was watching him. "The only thing would be to cut it off."

The lecturer was addressing an audience consisting mainly of women. The Ladies' Committee and college students sat on the front benches. There were a few fathers of families and a great many mothers, whilst several University students were also in the hall. Behind the speaker, and near an open door, stood a little group of Professors, who scanned the audience with attention.

Professor Goldworthy Fynes was delivering an introductory address. He had, up to the present time, declined to join his colleagues in their work at St. Mary's, owing, so it was said, to his fear lest contact with the inferior female intellect should narrow and deaden his own powers.

But repeated applications from the Council at St. Mary's and the prevailing influence of Minster had at length induced him to withdraw his refusal, and consent to lecture at St. Mary's Hall to a class of women.

Shortly after the arrival of Miss Crayston and Bertie Ravenshaw, it was announced that the dead lock with regard to the Latin classes was at an end, and that Professor Fynes would give an introductory address on the following Monday.

He had chosen for his title, "The Historical Attitude of Woman:" and Mrs. Brownlow said that the attitude, so far as she knew anything

about it, was chiefly remarkable because historical
women did not wear petticoats.

For more than an hour Mr. Fynes stooped over
his manuscript and tossed back his hair as he
descanted in very good English, but with a strongly-
marked French accent, upon the well-known and
universally-acknowledged inferiority of the female
sex throughout creation and from pre-historic
times. Brain power, nerve power, muscular power;
all of lower order. Intellect feeble, body frail.
Dependent for food and protection on the stronger
and more vigorous male. Not man, he assured
his hearers, but Nature, has stamped woman with
inferiority, and assigned her a position of subordination. He proceeded to lay down very
carefully his theory on the difference between the
sexes, warning his hearers that the very con-
ciseness which was characteristic of the masculine
grasp would probably cause it to be misunderstood; for women, he said, find it much easier to
catch at one or two words than to give patient
consideration to a consecutive argument. The
greatest thinker of the age, he continued, divides
our nature into three parts; the Feelings, the
Intellect, and the Character, corresponding to
Morality, Speculation, and Action.

At this point a slight diversion was created, for

the Professor went to a black board standing on an easel by his side, wrote these words with white chalk in large and very indistinct letters, and bracketed them.

This great thinker, he resumed, asserts the superiority of man in the two latter divisions; and in so doing he has the universal voice on his side. What is peculiar to him is, that he, as emphatically, asserts the superiority of woman in morality. Now it is one of Mr. Huxley's great objections to this theory that it does not admit the inferiority of woman on *all* points.

The Professor acknowledged that he, as an individual, certainly did think most English women not only deplorably uncultivated, but he also found that their attention was habitually directed to very frivolous and even degrading objects. On the other hand, he had seen American ladies who were decidedly superior to English ladies of the same natural capacity; therefore, as he could not presume to set up his own opinion in opposition to M. Comte or Mr. Huxley the two great authorities on this subject, he preferred for the present to suspend his judgment upon the inferiority of woman in the first division, namely, that of morality. In the other divisions there was a consensus of opinion throughout all ages. In

intellect and character, which correspond to speculation and action, her inferiority was univers-
ally recognised and acknowledged. The attempt,
therefore, of woman to storm a position closed
against her by natural laws was predestined to
failure, and certain to bring nothing but defeat
to the individual and degradation to humanity.
Her exclusion from active life, the result of
natural laws, acting unconsciously, would, as the
result of the labours of M. Comte, be formulated;
and would be in accordance with the theory
he had stated. This theory provided for the
happiness not merely of man, but of society.
For example, if Miss Emily Faithfull could open
the printing trade to women, the only result
would be that the same amount of capital which
now employs say a thousand men, would be
divided between a thousand men and a thousand
women; that is, instead of a man earning a guinea
a week for his family whilst the wife stays at
home, the labour of both would only earn a
guinea. All would suffer by such an arrangement, and the vital principle of the new creed
would be violated. "One of the most original and
fundamental doctrines of the new theory is," said
the Professor, "the following, which, in order to
impress it deeply upon the minds of those I see

before me, I will place upon the black board :"
and he wrote again in large and irregular letters :

"L'HOMME DOIT NOURRIR LA FEMME."

Mrs. Brownlow, who was on the front row of
seats, gazed at the inscription with interest, and
whispered to her cousin :

" Could almost believe I had seen it somewhere
before, dear ; couldn't you ? "

The half-audible murmur attracted the attention of the lecturer, who looked eagerly at Mrs.
Brownlow. He thought he had detected signs of
approval, and continued with increased energy :

" This is a fundamental condition ; and it is
thus that we legislate for women with a view to
the perfection of society, of which women form
half. There is for woman a loftier aim, a nobler
ideal, than mere success ; or than the rash attempt
to storm the position occupied by man, to share
his labours and rob him of his rewards. Look at
those points in which she excels. Women, for
example, are more religious than men ; we honour
them for it. They cling at present to theology,
which is a mere accident, theology being no
necessary element of religion ; but religion is
indispensable to the happiness of the individual
and the progress of the race. It is a terrible

thing," continued the Professor, in deep and
solemn tones, "that the principles of morality
on which our civilisation depends, should in
the popular mind be identified with forms of
religion which are every day becoming more dis-
credited. When every one in Europe believed
a theological dogma it was a very good basis on
which to build morality. But now-a-days, if
people are habituated to couple together the
divinity of a human being and moral duty, as
facts of equal certainty and importance, it will
go hard with the latter. It is to woman that we
look in this emergency. When she is introduced
to a new and purified form of belief, she will find
in it all the religion she wants, and will cling to
it with much more feeling than men. In fact,
for her is reserved a glorious mission. She will
become the instrument, as well as the object, of
man's worship. She may prepare herself to be
the worthy mate and intelligent companion of
the lofty being with whom she is associated. In
the pure and exalted air of subordination and
sacrifice, her noblest efforts will be crowned with
hitherto undreamed-of success. She will become
the companion and the friend of man, the mother
of the human young, and the material and moral
source of masculine energy."

The Professor ceased speaking. He took off his spectacles, wiped, replaced them, and looked keenly at the audience before him.

The ladies of the committee occupied the front row of chairs; but he looked beyond them to the large silent assemblage of women and girls, who appeared impressed and resigned.

"I thought there would have been more novelty in his views:" said one of the elder ladies to her neighbour; "I didn't care so very much for the lecture."

"Well, they are just my own opinions:" replied the person addressed, "but of course better expressed. Women should stay at home and attend to the house and their children."

"What he said about Roman Catholics," exclaimed one of the members of an evangelical congregation, "was really very beautifully put; that making human beings into saints and praying to them is the ruin of us."

"I didn't catch it. He speaks so fast and has such a curious pronunciation that I lost a good deal. Of course not, when he got angry and seemed as if he was going to chop off your head."

"I don't think I lost a syllable. Don't you remember his speaking of the superstition that degrades the present century, makes progress impossible, darkens the present, and threatens the future of the human race."

"No, indeed. That's very good. How can you remember it all?"

"Well, I wrote it down to show Mr. Early. He did not quite like me to come to the lecture. Professor Fynes was educated in France and has lived so much in Paris that Mr. Early considers him a very unsafe man. But any one who speaks like that about popery can't be far wrong."

"Did he mean popery?"

"Why what else could he mean?"

A warning hush — sh — sh — sh from the committee, and a scraping of chairs in the vicinity of the platform, notified to the talkers in different parts of the room that some one else was about to address the meeting.

There was a flutter of excitement in the front row as Professor Brownlow stepped upon the platform. Surely he would protest against the doctrine of woman's subordination! But no; he said he would not detain them a moment, took that opportunity of stating that the Greek class would be postponed from Wednesday to Friday, and would meet at the usual time and place.

Yes; that was all. He left the room without a

word in allusion to the lecture. There were murmurs of disapproval on the front row, and the name of Miss Kimberley Finch was handed along as if it had been a restorative.

"Presumptuous puppy:" exclaimed Miss le Mesurier, who occupied the last chair; and casting an indignant glance towards the back of the lecturer, she left the hall. Mrs. Milner sat with the tears streaming down her cheeks.

Mrs. Nicholl was trying to restrain Mrs. Brownlow, who said:

"Mary, I shall simply die if I don't; so let me go:" and she advanced.

"Mr. Fynes, I am going home to give my husband tea and toast, do come in as you pass the door. We shall be quite a family party; only Jack and me and the boy, and I do so want to ask you a few questions."

"Thank you, I never take tea."

"Well, I can give you milk. At this stage it forms the sole nourishment of the specimen of the human young which we keep on the premises."

There was an angry gleam in the Professor's eyes as he turned away from Mrs. Brownlow.

Mrs. Milner advanced:

"Oh, sir," she said, "shall I congratulate you

or condole with you. You have so much to learn."

Mr. Fynes stooped over the little white-haired lady, and looked benevolently, almost paternally, at her. He saw that she was troubled; and was pleased to discover that he had uprooted old superstitions, and prepared the way for a new and purer faith. He smiled, not as if anything external had moved him, but that smile which an inner consciousness of power brings to the surface.

"My lecture of to-day is the result," he said, "of an exhaustive study of the human race, with special reference to the functions of woman. On all other points I confess myself a student; but as to that I have nothing to learn."

"I will appeal to a student:" replied Mrs. Sturge, gazing upon him in dismay. "We will ask what effect your lecture has produced upon her. I am an old woman, and it does not matter what I think and feel; my only anxiety is for the dear girls I see about me."

Bertie Ravenshaw had passed round in front of the chairs on her way to the door. She bowed to Mrs. Milner, who stepped forward and laid her hand on the young girl's arm :

"Tell me, my love, did you like the lecture ?"

Mrs. Milner had seen Bertie several times at St. Mary's; but the manner in which she addressed her implied not intimacy, but an irresistible impulse of affection towards all young girls, which was characteristic of the childless widow.

Bertie blushed up to her hair as she replied:

"Oh, so much. I never heard anything so impressive."

The look of scorn with which the Professor had waited whilst Mrs. Milner made her appeal, faded from his face, and he turned to Bertie with evident interest and attention.

"Will it content you to be such a woman, in such a position as the Professor has described?"

"Indeed I fear I shall never be so good and noble; but I will try."

Mrs. Milner looked at her with amazement and the Professor with satisfaction. He bowed and turned away.

Bertie's blushes deepened. Mrs. Milner released her hand and sighed deeply. Bertie stood in silence for a few moments, and then, perceiving that Mrs. Milner was unconscious of her presence, she left the hall.

The young girl looked up to the sky as the eager March wind met her at the open door.

The clouds were sweeping rapidly from the west; heavy and dirty they looked as they passed on to the valley, but above them a deep serene blue gladdened her eyes. She turned away from the crowd about the gates of the college, and walked towards the park, a strip of undulating land along the summit of the cliffs. She saw nothing, however, as she walked, except the sky and the low, rapidly-moving clouds which hurried on, aimless, as it seemed, and troubled as her own thoughts.

She saw now for the first time what had been the lot of woman. She saw her crushed, dependent, humiliated, servile; taking the lowest place and the poorest portion, cursing the niggardly hand that bestowed only what it did not care to withhold, and hating the owner of it.

This was woman in the past. But now there was a new departure. Henceforward there was a possibility not merely of resignation and submission, but of acquiescence. To *choose* the lowest place; to take it, knowing what it is; not to be cajoled and flattered, but to accept with open eyes; to be despised and poor and oppressed, and to say : This is thy will, oh, my God, and it is mine. Surely this is right; surely it is Christ-like, thought Bertie; and then she saw that

this she could do ; abandon her own ambitious
dreams, her own highest aspirations for personal
well-being, and choose this lowly lot of self-
sacrifice.

It was thus that Bertie interpreted the lecture;
and she walked on rapidly, with beating heart
and heightened colour.

As she reached the cliff, strains of music from
the city fell upon her ear. A piano-organ drawn ·
by a pony and accompanied· by two men had
arrived in Minster. Once in every month or
five weeks it passed through the city. She had
seen it on the previous evening, and had been
informed that its advent was looked upon as an
event of much importance by all the children in
the place. She stood still to listen. Airs from
the Trovatore came to her amidst crash and
clatter. Music stirred her soul as with the call
of a trumpet. Unconsciously she kept time as
she walked, and turned her steps in the direction
of the sound. The wild, passionate pain of the
Verdi music, and the hopeless longing of it,
drew her onward and moved her with a strange
trouble. That *Non ti scordar di me* pierced her
like a sword; the life on which she had been
musing grew dim and cold and unlovely. She
left the heights, and, drawn towards the music

that had stirred her, she walked down to the
west gate of the old city.

As she passed beneath the gate the sound of
music was drowned by the cries and shouts of
men and boys in an adjacent street.   She
crossed the road and stood at the top of a steep
descent, on each side of which were low and
narrow houses festooned with dried fish and
haunted by many odours.   Half way down two
boys were fighting, and the noise proceeded from
an approving group of men and boys gathered
round them.   There was a moment's pause, and
Bertie saw two flushed and angry faces.   One boy
rubbed his nose with the palm of his hand, looked
ruefully at the blood, and seemed disposed to cry.

She walked swiftly down the steep descent
and marched into the midst of the group.

"Boys fighting like two wild animals!" she
said; "you ought to be ashamed of yourselves!
And to think of men standing by to watch these
miserable children and encourage them!"

"He begun it, miss," whimpered the boy with
the bleeding nose, whose tears started at Bertie's
first word; "he begun it, miss.   I shouldn't never
'ave said nothink to 'im."

"Never mind who began it.   You are going
to end it now.   Come with me:" and she took a

hand which he seemed by no means unwilling to give. "I'll have no fighting; and I'm downright ashamed to see grown men stand by and encourage boys to fight and kick as I saw you doing."

Bertie stood erect as a grenadier and looked her men full in the face.

Two or three of them slouched away with their hands in their pockets, and whistled, but not very loud.

"Well, I'm dormed!" said one great fellow, with the brevity and directness of his class. "And pray, miss, who may you be?"

Bertie faced round towards the speaker and looked him straight in the eyes.

"Come on, Bob:" said a companion, dragging him away, "'tain't o' no use to argy."

Bertie was of the same mind; and a few moments later, when the crowd had dispersed, she took the boy, whose hand she still held, with her to the top of the street.

A voice close to her said gravely:

"I thought I recognised you, Miss Ravenshaw, and I was coming towards you. I am afraid you do not know the character of some of these streets. This is one that it is not safe for a lady to enter. There are very rough people about."

"I'm not in the least afraid of boys:" replied

Bertie. "I'm accustomed to them; and I cannot keep my hands off when they are fighting.
It is such a brutal thing. I've brought this one
away, you see; and when his nose stops bleeding
and he leaves off crying I shall give him a penny
and a scolding."

"But those boys were in the midst of men of
the lowest class; rough, seafaring fellows, and
many of them foreigners."

"Oh, I *am* glad to hear they are not English.
They ought to be ashamed of themselves; and I
think they must be. They must feel what a
disgrace it is that I should have to separate these
little fellows. Why you are not ten years old,
are you?" asked Bertie of her prisoner.

"Yes, I am:" sulkily. "I'm turned twelve."

"Poor child! And they were calling out,
'Go it, my game chicken!' I'm sure there
isn't much game in him, though there seems a
good deal of chicken."

The boy looked cowed and humbled; and
Bertie, whose excitement had overcome her
habitual reserve with strangers, said to Mr.
Brownlow:

"I mustn't stop. I know what boys are.
They hate getting a preachment, and it will be of
no use to say much or to keep him long."

CHAPTER IX.

BERTIE IN THE CLASS-ROOM.

WHEN Mr. Fynes left the lecture-hall he paused
for a moment at a door on which "Office" was
painted in white letters. He looked at the
lecture he had just delivered, and which he held
in his hand, a goodly mass of manuscript, and
after a moment's hesitation entered. Miss Crayston sat at one end of a long table, with books
and papers before her; girls came and went on
their errands to ask questions and consult her
about books. A door communicating with the
library was open, and through it came a hum of
voices, probably from the general waiting-room
which was beyond the library, and the door leading into which was also open.

"You will find the Greek lexicon on the
second shelf to the left:" said Miss Crayston to a
small pale woman who had come for information.
"And will you kindly close the door into the

waiting-room. There is so much talking that I fear the readers will be disturbed."

At this moment Mr. Fynes entered the room.

"The students have come down from your lecture," said Miss Crayston, "and seem to be discussing it somewhat eagerly."

"Were you present?" he asked, going up to her and steadily gazing at the brown glossy hair.

"No; I am unable to leave the office during the day."

"If the subject is one that interests you I shall be glad to lend you my manuscript. I propose ultimately to publish, but it may be some time before I am able to amplify and prepare for the press."

"Thank you; I should like to see it."

"I think you were present, Walmsley, were you not?" said Mr. Fynes, addressing the Professor of Mathematics, who was in the position he ordinarily occupied in every room which he entered, namely, sitting before the fire with his feet on the fender.

"Yes, I was."

"Have you studied the 'Philosophie Positive'?"

"No, but I think I have done as much as any of the disciples of Comte. I have bought all his books."

K 2

" Have you read them ? "

" If I had I should have done more than most
of the disciples : " replied Mr. Walmsley, not
without malice. He did not approve of loans to
the Lady Resident, nor of his colleague's steadfast
gaze.

Mr. Fynes was about to answer when Miss le
Mesurier entered from the library.

" I have just come from the waiting-room : "
she said in her harshest tones, looking ferocious,
and glancing suspiciously at the heap of manuscript lying before Miss Crayston, " and I must
say, Mr. Fynes, that the women in this college
are not at all prepared for the *subordination* you
advocate. I never knew a lecture give so much
offence."

Mr. Fynes was a vain man, and keenly touched
by the slightest hint of disapprobation. He was
eager to resent the disappointment caused by
the unfavourable reception of his lecture, and
replied with severity :

" I used the term ' subordination ' in its philosophical sense. If my hearers are unable to
understand me I am indifferent to their opinion,
and have nothing more to say to them."

" I suppose you are not quite indifferent to the
view that the managers and the council may take."

" I am profoundly indifferent to it."

" Pray may I ask on what ground?" inquired Miss le Mesurier in a tone and with a manner which went far to justify almost any answer she might receive.

" There are some persons," he replied, speaking angrily and rapidly, " whom I consider it worth pleasing or inspiring with respect for me, because I respect them, or like them, or admire them. But there are a great many persons whom I either positively despise or dislike, or for whose opinion I feel a perfect indifference. I should get on much better in the world if I systematically conciliated this large class, which includes all those persons whom I do not intimately know, and a great many of those whom I do; but it really is too exhausting. It is like being always at work."

Miss le Mesurier made no answer. She left the room hurriedly. Miss Crayston stooped low over her books, and Mr. Walmsley put both hands through the short thick red hair which grew straight up all over his head. He had risen from his chair and was standing with his back to the fire. His mouth was grave, and the lips, as usual, compressed; but his light-blue eyes danced with something that looked very like a smile.

After a moment's silence he said to Miss
Crayston, who also smiled when her eyes met
his :

"Has my class gone up ?"

"The bell has not yet rung, it wants two
minutes to the time. May I tell Miss Ravenshaw that you will see her ?"

"Of course, if you really desire it. You know
that my rule is to receive no new pupils during
the session."

"But you will make an exception in her
favour if she is fit to join either of your classes ?"

"Certainly ; but it is most unlikely. Oh,
there's the bell : " and he walked to the door ; then
looking back, he added : "There's a little table
by the window ; tell her to come up in an hour's
time with the junior division, and to sit there."

Before the time indicated Bertie had returned.
She went into the office and laid a bunch of
spring violets by the side of Miss Crayston.

"They are the first I have seen," she said ;
"and they are so sweet that I could not resist
them."

"Thanks, Bertie. First violets are an event
in the year. I am glad to see you, for I was
afraid you would be late."

"I have no class this afternoon."

"Yes; you are to go up to Mr. Walmsley with the juniors."

"Oh, thank you. It is the very thing I desire."

"There is the bell. Just leave your hat in the dressing-room, go up at once, and sit at the visitors' table in the window."

Bertie complied, and a moment later entered the class-room. It was oblong, large, and lofty; lighted at one end by a bow window, opposite to which, at the far end of the room, was a black board. The Professor stood with his back to the class and was writing on the board when the new pupil entered. Eleven girls lifted their heads to look at her, and one of them caught her dress as she passed and whispered:

"You have come into the wrong room."

Bertie did not reply. She took the seat which had been indicated and waited.

The Professor looked at her from time to time and hesitated. He was not aware that the tall, beautiful girl whom he had frequently noticed, was the pupil on whose behalf Miss Crayston had interceded. For a few minutes he was sorry for himself. One lovely woman was already troubling his peace, and he was disposed to think that officials ought not to be lovely women with lovely

pupils and any number of possible lovers. He
liked pupils to be pupils and not lovely women ;
and he looked with complacency at the desks
before him and the studious faces above them.
Whatever else could be said of the class the
disturbing element of female loveliness was certainly absent. He was not nervous with a pupil,
whether man or woman ; but something of the
nervousness that beset him in private life, and
when he was with Miss Crayston, made him
linger as he approached Bertie, and stop to
arrange the pens in a tray on the desk and stoop
to pick up a sheet of paper. When he was close
to her, and the earnest grey eyes were fixed on
him, and her colour went and came, his confidence returned :

"Do you know anything of mathematics ?" he
asked.

"Very little. Perhaps I had better say nothing. I have worked quite alone."

"Have you got Euclid's 'Elements' ?"

"No ; the copy I used was my brother's, so
I could not bring it away."

"Do you know the axioms and postulates ?"

"Yes ; and the first book and the third."

The Professor looked at her with an amused
twinkle in his eyes :

" Oh, you know the first book and the third ?
Can you remember them ? "

" Yes."

" Could you write out two or three problems
from memory ? "

" Yes."

He took three sheets of paper, and at the top
of each scrawled in pencil an irregular figure.

" Can you make out the letters ? "

" Not very well."

" Then I will tell you. You will soon get
accustomed to my writing."

Bertie opened a case she had brought with
her and took out compasses, an ivory ruler, and
fine pointed pen.

The Professor watched her with a smile.

" What are you going to do ? "

" Draw the diagrams."

" No, no ; I don't want that. Just write out
the proof here, under my figures, they will do
very well, and use my letters ; and so saying he
turned and left her.

Bertie gazed upon the sheets before her in
dismay. Mr. Walmsley returned to the black
board and his demonstrations. From time to time
he eyed her keenly as she sat with both elbows
on the table, and her head between her hands,

gazing first at one and then at another of the three
sheets. But he did not return until the class
was dismissed. He saw that she was unable to
execute the task he had assigned, and did not
wish to accentuate her failure.

At last he approached :

" Well, you can't get on ? I didn't expect you
could ; and you see it would be impossible for me
to go back over old ground, so you had better
wait and come to me next October."

Bertie blushed and was horribly nervous, but
she contrived to say : "I do know those books
and these particular problems quite well."

" Then why can't you write them out ? "

" Because M N ought to be equal to V S, and
O P to L R, but they are none of them of the
same length ; and the circles O E M and X Y Z
ought to be equal, and the angles at their centres
equal, but this is not so ; indeed the figures are
not circles at all. The pentagon, too, is neither
equilateral nor equiangular."

The Professor looked keenly at her, and saw
by her face that the difficulty was a real one :

" And so you think that because I don't draw
an accurate diagram the principles embodied in
the argument are incorrect."

" I don't quite understand you."

"Don't you see there is an abstract truth which these forms embody, but which is not identical with them. Can't you reason out from an ideal which my crooked lines recall, though they do not represent it."

Bertie's eyes drooped :

"I am ashamed:" she said. "You see how ignorant I am. I never looked beyond the mere figure on the paper before me."

She bowed her head, but he could see the burning blushes which coloured brow and ears, and he was sorry for her.

"Could you have written out these problems if you had used my letters and drawn your own diagrams ?"

"Yes."

"Very well. Do it now. I will wait."

It cost Bertie a great effort, but she looked up and said earnestly :

"If you will allow me to use your diagrams I will try to show you——" but she broke down in her little speech, and could only falter out : "I am so sorry; I have been very stupid. I didn't understand. Do give me one more chance."

"To be sure :" he replied kindly ; "and I will try to improve my scrawling figures."

He was about to take them, but Bertie laid her two hands on the papers.

"Ah, please don't touch them:" she exclaimed. "Do let me have them just as they are."

"Very well! Don't hurry. I have some work, and can do it here."

He took a chair to the fireplace, which was on one side of the room, and began to look over the papers given by his class, and to correct them in pencil. From time to time he glanced towards Bertie. She wrote steadily on, without raising her eyes. He smiled as he watched her; for the relation of master and pupil once established, all his nervous shyness vanished. He had at any rate found a pupil who interested him, and he half rose as he saw her lay aside the second page and take up the third and last; but he decided not to interrupt her, and resumed his own work.

The door of the room opened and Mrs. Armstrong entered. She gave a very obvious start of surprise and said: " Do I interrupt you, Mr. Walmsley?"

"My class is not over:" he replied, frigidly, rising from his chair.

"Oh, indeed. I thought I heard the bell half-an-hour ago."

Mr. Walmsley said nothing, but continued to

make marginal notes on a paper which he held in his hand, as he stood facing Mrs. Armstrong. She looked uneasily towards Bertie, who did not so much as lift her eyes. Under these circumstances, after watching them both for five minutes, she left the room, and shortly afterwards returned with her work-bag. She placed a chair by the side of the black board, a position which commanded the whole room, fetched a footstool, and taking out a long strip of white embroidery stitched in silence. Professor Walmsley fidgeted. He walked from the fireplace to the table, and then to the window, and stood before Bertie. She looked up at him with her clear, frank eyes and said :

" Only a few more lines."

He made no reply, but took up the two finished papers and glanced over them ; then he took the third from her hand and inspected that also.

" Very good :" he said ; " quite right."

Mrs. Armstrong cleared her throat and rose from her chair. He added hastily :

" This class is of no use to you. Come up with the senior division next Tuesday. Miss Crayston will get the work for you from some one in the class."

He left the room hurriedly, taking the papers with him.

Mrs. Armstrong approached the window; and before she had · decided what to say, Bertie bowed and passed out at the door.

The manager stood irresolute and angry. She had wanted to say something, and had not known exactly what it was to be, or how she should begin.

Bertie, as she passed the office, saw that Miss Crayston was alone, and going in she stooped over her and whispered: "Mrs. Armstrong is up-stairs. She looks like a district visitor who has a tract to deliver. I rushed away."

Meanwhile, as Mrs. Armstrong stood in the empty room looking at Bertie's vacant seat, Miss le Mesurier entered.

"There are violets on the office table," she said in a half-whisper to her friend; "but I can't make out if it was Fynes that brought them or Walmsley."

CHAPTER X.

A PRACTICAL JOKE.

"BERTIE, will you put away your books and talk to me for half-an-hour?"

"Oh, please, let me have a little more time."

"That is what you always say. However, I know you are very busy to-day, and we will talk some other time; I will ring for your lamp, you must not try your eyes in this half-light."

"No, no; that will never do. My work is very delightful, but you are better than everything:" and the girl rose from a table at the window where she was writing, opened a drawer, put away books and papers, and springing across the room threw herself on the hearth-rug at Miss Crayston's feet, and clasped her hands upon that lady's knees, saying:

"You see, I am so happy; and whatever I am doing I could go on doing for ever."

"I am sorry for that."

" Why ? "

" Because just now you are sitting on the floor."

Bertie blushed as she said :

" I wonder what it is that makes me do the very thing that I have ridiculed in others. I never saw any grown person sit on the floor until we were at Mrs. Goodall's the other night, and you know how I laughed at that absurd, sentimental Minnie Pearson, who went about the room kneeling first before one lady and then another, until finally she reclined at Mrs. Brownlow's feet and looked up into her eyes.

" I saw Minnie jump up with a very red face. What did Mrs. Brownlow say to her ? "

> " ' Twinkle, twinkle, little star,
> How I wonder what you are : '

and it really was rather hard upon Minnie. She is such a very little star."

" Well, Bertie, why do you do the same thing ? "

" Can't help it. It never occurred to me to do it before ; but sitting here at your feet is just where I ought to be ; and I won't clasp my hands, or twist my head, or turn my eyes up, so please let me for this one night."

" This room is quite comfortable : " she continued. "And yet what a dreary place it looked when we first came to it. Now, in the evening when we see the sunset glow in the sky, or at night when you sit by the fire with your little table and the green lamp, it is like a picture, and I hear music."

"What do you mean?"

"Don't you know when one sees anything very beautiful how the music comes, sometimes grave and sad, sometimes bright and cheerful. Each thing has its own."

"No; I don't know that at all; but I should like to know what kind of music you associate with me."

"Something so strange," said Bertie; "and yet it is always that or something very like it. Do you know the grand, solemn Funeral March in Beethoven's 12th Sonata? I hear the distant sounds, the tramp of many feet, the clang of arms, and there are loud shouts, cries of exultation, the firing of distant guns. Then out of all the darkness bursts a triumphal strain, the song of victory, victory in spite of pain and sorrow and loss, and that is *you*."

"Thanks, dear:" said Miss Crayston, with an attempt to smile, but her lips trembled. "I think I am very cruel to you, Bertie, not to get a piano."

"Not at all. Didn't I tell you I had resolved to give up music?"

"No; may I ask why."

"Well, you see, it's of no use to do a little of a great many things. I am sure that is the way in which girls fritter away their time and do no good after all; so I have resolved to work hard at just a few things whilst I am at college. I do love music so very much that it always tempts me away from other studies, and it might make me neglect my duty. When I first came I really pined for it. Ever since I can remember I have fallen asleep to the sound of music, for at home my bed-room is above the drawing-room. I miss the home music more than anything else, except," in a low voice, "my father."

"Are they all musical at home?"

"Nearly all. You would really be astonished to hear Lizzie play. You know she's not clever. Oh, not at all. In fact, I don't consider her even very intelligent. She certainly has no intellectual tastes, and yet she can play Schubert and Chopin in the most wonderful manner. That is one reason why I intend to give up music. I think it goes with rather a low order of intellect, don't you?"

Miss Crayston looked amused, and did not answer.

"There, now!" exclaimed Bertie, starting to her feet. "I have been saying something awfully conceited. I know it by your face. Don't tell me what it is. I know quite well."

"Don't be unhappy, Bertie. When a sense of your own superiority comes outside in that innocent way it is very easy to get rid of it."

"Superiority, indeed! Well, I have deserved it. But I wish you would tell me why, when I was at home, I never used to forget what an ignorant dunce I was; whilst I never think of it now that I am in the midst of learned people. If one of these Professors had so much as lifted his hat to me a year ago I should have been unspeakably proud and happy at the mere recognition of my existence; and now I am quite calm when he listens to me with respectful attention."

"I imagine that the way in which any man behaves to a woman depends not so much on her as on himself."

"I know what you mean, and I am learning to see the same thing. There's ever so much shoddy among the students, I mean the cap and gown ones, and you can tell it directly by the way they behave to the girls and women. They are bold and insolent whenever they can try it on."

"May I ask what shoddy means?"

"Oh, don't you know? Not the real genuine article, but something made up of refuse and rags."

"The shoddy students will not be grateful for the name."

"It's a very good name for them. I didn't invent it. My father detests shoddy, and I have learnt to recognise and dislike it from him. Now there is not a morsel of shoddy among the Professors. They are kings and princes, every one of them:" said Bertie, with enthusiasm. "There is not one of them who could do a discourteous act, or say an ungracious word, to any girl, however stupid or ill-born and bred she may be."

"I think you are right, Bertie. It is this that fits them for their task, and that has possibly helped them to undertake it."

Bertie had fallen into that state of rapturous admiration for a woman, which is not uncommon amongst women. Instead of replying to Miss Crayston's last remark she stooped and kissed her hands, saying:

"You don't know how happy I am, here, and with you. If I could only help to make you happy I should be contented. Do tell me what they say and do at the committee meetings."

Miss Crayston started at this unexpected speech.

"That is not a discreet question, Bertie."

"Isn't it? Then I am sorry that I asked. You always look anxious before the meetings and worried afterwards, and there are notes coming all day long."

"I did not know I had such an observant companion."

"Is it wrong? I cannot help it. How is it possible to avoid knowing you are troubled when your face shows it so clearly?"

"There is nothing, Bertie, that I can tell you:" replied Miss Crayston kindly. "The management and direction of the college are not easy things. We are all naturally anxious to arrange everything in the best way, and I am new to the work. No doubt I have made many blunders, and committed many faults."

"That I am sure you have not:" exclaimed Bertie, hotly.

"Well, I won't attempt to prove my assertion:" replied Miss Crayston. "By the way, I must answer one of those notes this evening; and here is an invitation from Mrs. Armstrong, which you may answer for me if you will."

"You won't accept it?" exclaimed Bertie.

" Yes; I think we had better do so."

" Very well; of course I shall go if you do : " responded Bertie, but not very cheerfully; and then she broke into a merry laugh.

" I know it is idiotic to laugh in this way," she said, " but it comes of an unfortunate habit I have got of seeing things instead of thinking of them. Just then I saw a particularly ugly, ill-natured old woman, who is in my mother's district. She has always a long story to tell to the discredit of her neighbours, and at some point of it she invariably says : ' Saving your presence, mum.' When she reaches that stage my mother sends away whichever of us happens to be with her. One day we insisted on being told what comes after ' Saving your presence,' and mother said it was always something very disagreeable to listen to."

" Well ?"

" Oh," continued Bertie, with some hesitation, " I don't think you'll like me to go on; and I wish I hadn't begun. The fact is, I am afraid I was thinking those notes of Mrs. Armstrong's and Miss le Mesurier's ought to commence, ' Saving your presence, mum,' instead of ' Dear Miss Crayston.' "

Miss Crayston's head was bent down, and she made no reply.

" Beg your pardon, mum," said Gibson, who suddenly appeared with his white face set in the gloom of Miss Crayston's doorway, " but there's a lady a-settin' afore the fire in the ladies' cloak-room."

" Leastways afore the fireplace, for fire there is none," added his wife, peeping over his shoulder ; " and she've got her feet stuck on the fender."

Miss Crayston looked up and said :

" Mrs. Armstrong came about three o'clock, and went to one of the class-rooms. She fetched a book from the library, which I have not seen her bring back. She is probably reading, and as there is very little to be done in the room I think, Mrs. Gibson, you may leave it to the morning."

" Lor, mum : " exclaimed Mrs. Gibson, pushing her husband on one side so as also to appear in the doorway, " it worn't my work as I was a-thinkin' of, that can stand over well enough. But 'tain't Mrs. Armstrong as is a-settin' there. She's got a libery book on her lap, sure enough, for I can see the ticket on it; but she ain't stirred this two hours, not when I stood at the door and coughed."

Bertie rose from her usual seat at the window, and coming forward, said :

"I think Mrs. Armstrong brought a lady with her, Miss Crayston. Nora Stewart told me there were two bonnets and shawls in that room, and after Mrs. Armstrong had gone Nora said the door was ajar, and a lady was sitting near the fireplace reading."

Miss Crayston looked at Bertie with some surprise; and Bertie, going close to her, said in a low tone so as not to be heard by the Gibsons,

"The girls in the waiting-room were all talking about it, so you need not be astonished at my gossip; the fact is, there was a regular outburst of indignation. They thought Mrs. Armstrong had set some one to watch them. One of them went up quietly and shut the door, but ten minutes later they said it was open again, and the strange lady was sitting there with her book."

Miss Crayston called to mind the complaints of talking in the general waiting-room which Mrs. Armstrong had made that afternoon. She had said how much it annoyed the ladies, whose little cloak-room was on the opposite side of the passage. Miss Crayston had urged that it was undesirable, and would be very difficult, to interfere in the matter; that when the door of communication with the library was closed such noise as there was could annoy no one; that it

was natural there should be a buzz of voices
when the classes were over; and that as the ladies
did not sit in their cloak-room she was sure they
would not wish to place any unnecessary restrictions upon the students. Mrs. Armstrong had
replied somewhat angrily, that the ladies very probably would make much more use of their room
than they hitherto had done. Recalling this conversation Miss Crayston did not feel any alarm
at the report respecting the motionless figure.
She said, "You had better wait a little longer,
Mrs. Gibson, and then if the lady is still here you
can go in and say that the college closes at four,
and it is now after six. Ask her if she will sit
in the waiting-room, as she will find it more
comfortable. I have no doubt Mrs. Armstrong will
return, and that this lady is waiting on business."

Gibson and his wife still stood in the doorway,
and Mrs. Gibson, clutching her husband's arm,
said :

"Lor, mum, I wouldn't go a-nigh her, not if you
was to offer me untold gold ; and Gibson's afraid
of his life of a corpse."

"A corpse, Mrs. Gibson, how can you talk
such nonsense !"

"'Tain't no nonsense :" said the little woman,
bursting into tears; "for I can see the face quite

plain through her veil, leastwise her nose, and
it's the face of the dead, that's what it is."

Miss Crayston rose to leave the room, and
Bertie sprang to her side:

"I would much rather go alone, Bertie dear; I
will send for you if necessary, but please stay
here till I return."

Gibson and his wife drew back, and Miss
Crayston preceded them to the ladies' cloak-room.
She paused for a moment at the door, and saw a
stooping figure sitting near the fireplace. She
spoke, but received no answer. She stepped
forward, and discerned a large, white, and very
prominent feature underneath the veil; and then
the Lady Resident smiled. She took hold of the
bonnet, the figure suddenly collapsed, and Mrs.
Gibson uttered a loud shriek.

Bertie had resumed her seat at the window;
but when she heard the cry she hurried to the
cloak-room, where she found Gibson kneeling by
the side of his wife and crying, Mrs. Gibson in
hysterics, and Miss Crayston trying to make her
lie on the floor. Two or three umbrellas, a bonnet attached to them by a string, and a heap of
books, cloaks, and shawls, on the chair by the
fireplace, revealed the nature of the trick that
had been played.

Bertie fetched a tumbler of water, dashed it in Mrs. Gibson's face, and in the momentary silence that ensued she said :

" Now, Mrs. Gibson, don't be foolish. It's all a joke. You can see there is nothing the matter. Some one has made a scarecrow out of the umbrellas and cloaks. That's all."

The poor woman gave one pitiful glance at Bertie and fainted, whereupon that damsel desired the husband to carry his wife to the parlour; but seeing that he trembled too violently to be trusted to do anything, she and Miss Crayston lifted Mrs. Gibson, and bore her to their little sitting-room.

Bertie administered sal-volatile, helped Mrs. Gibson to her room, and got her to bed; sat by her side and made her laugh over the joke of the dressed-up figure until the tears ran down her cheeks, and finally left her in good spirits, but very much ashamed of having been so foolish and given so much trouble.

" Miss Bertie," said Gibson, when they were left alone, " is what I call a Nero."

" Lor, James, she seems to me much more of the hangel unawares. But there, I don't like to say more in favour of one than of another; for all the time Miss Crayston sat here so quiet she was

a-holding my hand, which for all the world is like
the back of a nutmeg-grater, in one of them little
white, soft hands of hern, and somehow it seemed
to soothe me and quieten me more than words
can tell.   Who was it as wanted 'er just now ? "

" One of them himpious old cats, you may be
sure."

" Mercy sakes, James, don't talk like that !   I
can't abide to hear you swear."

" Well, they're enough to make a man swear.
A pretty row there'll be to-morrow."

" What about ! "

" Why about all this here rumpus—"

" You never told 'em nothin', did you ? "

" They never wants no tellin' ; they ferrets
things out."

" Dear, dear," said Mrs. Gibson with a sigh.
" I wouldn't get the young ladies into a scrape
was it ever so, and you can't tell but what our
Miss Bertie may be in it ; for after all gals will
be gals, just as boys will be boys."

" Well, they'll get nothin' out of me : " said
Gibson.

" Nor me neither : " said his wife ; " and if they
says anything to me about bein' took bad to-night,
I'll at 'em about making me get up at four this
morning to scrub them rooms.   Miss Crayston

never **knowed** nothin' about it; and when she come down at seven and see me she went an' got me a cup of tea with her own hands, that she did, and sit by and made me take it. She have got a proud sperrit, James; and she's a real lady, and no mistake. She won't demean herself to say nothin' to me; but lor', what a life they do lead her."

CHAPTER XI.

RIVAL POWERS.

BERTIE and Miss Crayston returned to the sitting-room and discussed the events of the evening.

" You have had more experience in hysterics and fainting than has fallen to my lot, Bertie :" said Miss Crayston.

" I should think so. We never do it ourselves, I mean in the family, but among the maids there are generally two or three who scream and faint. There was one used to scream at beetles, and, as we could not get rid of them, my mother had to forbid her to go into the kitchen; another fainted at skinned rabbits; and the majority of girls in the lower orders sit down and turn white at the sight of blood."

" Another of your sweeping generalisations, Bertie."

" No ; really there is something in it this time.

My father thinks that the state of health which
goes with this tendency is the result of early
hardship, poverty, and want of good nourishing
food; comprehensive ignorance has also a good
deal to say to it. Mrs. Gibson will be all right
to-morrow, and you need not be uneasy. I
wonder who dressed up that figure."

"It was very cleverly done. I was quite
taken in by it at first; and if the nose had been
a little less pronounced I should really have
been startled."

"Was there a nose? what was it made of?"

"The ivory handle of your umbrella."

"My umbrella! Why I have lost it since
Saturday!"

"Yes; and I have now found nearly all the
shawls and water-proofs, even the overshoes, that
have been missing; it was those large feet on the
fender that deceived Mrs. Gibson."

"Then it has been planned for some time,"
said Bertie, "for some of those things have been
lost more than a week. I wonder where they
have been hidden."

"So do I:" replied Miss Crayston. "Miss le
Mesurier came," she continued, "whilst we were
both with Mrs. Gibson, and has discovered the
whole thing. I tell her it is a foolish joke, and

that it will be well to take very little notice of it; but she insists on it being investigated."

"Investigated!" echoed Bertie. "Oh, I am sorry!"

"Why?"

"Because I am afraid I know who it is. At least I ought not to say that, but I suspect some one. You need have no fear:" she added, hastily, "I could not speak even to you of my suspicions."

"Quite right, Bertie dear; and I still hope that Miss le Mesurier may be influenced by my advice, and take very little notice of this freak. It should be treated as a childish matter, unworthy even of grave reprobation."

But Mrs. Armstrong and Miss le Mesurier were not at all influenced by Miss Crayston's advice. On the contrary, they placarded the class-rooms with remonstrances in the first place, and then with appeals to the students to name the "guilty parties," who must be known to some of them.

Bertie entered the office one day when Miss Crayston was alone and said indignantly:

"I wish we had my father here."

"Why?"

"Because he hates a tale-bearer. He will allow no tale-bearing in school or out of it, and now I see how right he is. Nothing can be more demoralising than to try and make girls betray a companion. All the girls here with any sense of honour and justice are furious; and the sneaks are in and out of the ladies' cloak-room all day long, accusing every one they can think of."

Miss Crayston made no reply, and Bertie continued with a flaming face :

" I have been sent for this afternoon and asked to ' account for the presence of my umbrella.' I really didn't at first know what Mrs. Armstrong meant. I thought it was a joke; and when I did understand I merely replied that I could not account for it in any way, and that I had mislaid the umbrella almost a week previously. They allowed me to see very plainly that they did not believe a word I said, and I left the room."

" It is a wretched affair : " said Miss Crayston ; " and the ladies insist on managing it their own way. But I really think I must go into the waiting-room and speak to the students myself."

" Oh, pray do ! " exclaimed Bertie. " You will set everything right ; I know you will. Come in now. The girls have nearly all come down from the class-rooms ; I will soon get them together, and say you want to speak to them. Do come."

Miss Crayston hesitated. She was very loyal to the council under which she worked, and would not oppose any member of it so long as it could be helped. But these particular members were doing harm instead of good; moreover, the "investigation" was, as they had assured her, as much her duty as theirs, and she saw that the time had come when she ought to carry it out in her own way.

"I will be with you in five minutes:" she said to Bertie, who hurried off at this announcement, and returned within the specified time to announce that the room was quite full. Miss Crayston followed her, and took her place at one end, near the fireplace, where Bertie had secured a vacant space by means of a barrier of chairs.

"Miss Crayston is going to speak to us:" she had said in her clear ringing tones; and all were silent, and made way for the Lady Resident as she passed through their midst.

Bertie was bright, eager, and happy; very proud of the achievement of getting Miss Crayston "on her feet," and confident that the mountain would prove to be a molehill as soon as the light shone on it.

Miss Crayston was paler than usual; and her voice, clear, low, resonant, had that thrill of emotion, that sound as of the beating of a heart, which secured interest and attention from every one present. It cost her a great effort to speak aloud to this room full of girls and women. There were fifty or sixty present, of ages ranging from sixteen to five or six-and-thirty, and Miss Crayston was one of those women who can speak with ease to one or two listeners only. She hesitated for a moment, and then began :

"I want to speak to you about something you will all have heard of ; and before I speak about it I should like to clear away some misapprehensions which may have arisen in your own minds concerning it. Of course you know that I allude to the construction of a scarecrow in the ladies' cloak-room."

There was a general laugh at the use of the word *scarecrow*, and a rustle among the audience, who gathered closer to the speaker ; whilst those at the remote end of the room stood on chairs, in order to see her distinctly.

"I want to tell you that I don't think any grave fault has been committed ; indeed I doubt whether I should call it a fault at all. If that figure had been built up by children we should all have considered it a capital joke, and very cleverly carried out. It really was a most life-like thing. Any girl or boy under fourteen might well have been proud of it. Above that age I should call it an outbreak of childish folly to dress a scarecrow, but really I see no harm in it, even then. Many girls from sixteen to nineteen years old would consider it a bit of fun to make their companions think a lady was sitting in a chair reading a book, when there was nothing there but a few umbrellas and some cloaks. Above twenty I imagine no one but an idiot could take any pleasure in such an entertainment."

There was a laugh at this statement, and the elder listeners, who had shown signs of irritation when Miss Crayston began to speak, were mollified.

"There are no children in St. Mary's and no idiots:" continued the Lady Resident, "so we know that the trick has been played by some young girl who thought it a bit of fun; and I do hope you will not allow it to assume the importance and magnitude of an offence. It is true that this figure was dressed up in the ladies' cloak-room; but as it was first seen after college hours, and when the ladies of the committee had left, there can have been no intention either to annoy or to ridicule them."

Miss Crayston looked round as she said these words, which were received with warm approval.

"I am sorry," she resumed, "to be compelled to allude to a notion which would reflect discredit of a grave kind on many of you; but I know that it has gained ground, and therefore we had better speak of it and set it aside. I think you will agree with me that some young girl has played a practical joke of a most innocent kind, in fact so innocent as to be childish."

There was a murmur at the word "innocent," which Miss Crayston heard and understood.

"I know," she said, "to what you allude; the porter's wife was frightened; she fainted, and was ill with headache all the following day. But it was not the intention of our unknown friend to frighten the porter's wife; and although her illness gives us good reason to say that such jokes should never be encouraged or even tolerated, we must not allow ourselves to attribute unmerited blame and to censure as cruel a girl who was only heedless. In fact, 'young and foolish' is my verdict, and she won't do it again."

Bertie's beaming face was a pleasure to see. Miss Crayston gathered courage as she proceeded and spoke slowly, but with great fluency.

She carried her audience with her; and Bertie, to her intense delight, saw that they were considering the subject in a very different frame of mind to that which prevailed when the Lady Resident began to speak.

"No grave fault has been committed," continued Miss Crayston, "none that cannot be, and will not be, easily overlooked by us all; but I wish to put it to my *young* friends," and she laid special emphasis on the *young*, "is it a brave or a right thing to allow any one else to receive blame, great or small, which you deserve? If you are bold enough to play a trick should you not have the courage to avow it? Is it quite what I expect of you? Is it honourable to allow the girls whose cloaks and umbrellas you took to carry out your joke, to be cross-questioned and even suspected, until this foolish affair assumes almost the aspect of a crime?"

As the Lady Resident spoke her voice trembled, and she added very slowly:

"I shall be much obliged if whoever dressed the figure will tell me of it herself. I will not listen to any charge brought against another."

"Sure and you're right," said a bright-haired Irish girl with a large flat rosy face, an upturned nose, and laughing eyes, who started up as the

Lady Resident ceased speaking. "You're just as right as rain; an' it was me that dressed up the bogie, an' so the murder's out, an' there's an end of it. I never thought there'd be such a fuss and all, over it. I did it myself; and if you want to find the rest of the things they're in that empty cistern over the door."

"Thank you, Nora:" said Miss Crayston; "thank you very much for removing undeserved suspicion."

"Three cheers for Nora Stewart:" cried Bertie, and there was much laughing and some cheering; but Nora said with a comical face:

"You may laugh and cheer as much as you like, but it's more than I shall do. I'd have told long ago, but I knew I should be worried out of my loife by one and another of them."

"Who is she?" was asked by some present.

"Oh, don't you know? We used to call her the wild Irish girl when she first came from Belfast. She is one of the boarders under Miss Flint."

"Poor thing!"

Miss Crayston was speaking earnestly to Nora. The girl had become rather pale; she replied:

"Now don't you trouble about it, Miss Crayston.

I shall always be proud to know I've pleased you.
And you're just roight about everything. It was
a bit of fun, and I meant to poke the old creature
down when they were all gone ; but jest as I was
at the door Miss Flint called me and I had to go
away. Don't you mind anything she may say.
I'd have told long before if I'd known you cared
about it."

A small slight woman with a grey face, grey
eyes, and grey hair in stiff corkscrew curls, had
approached unnoticed as Nora was speaking.

"You will come with me, Miss Stewart, immediately :" she said; and Nora, with a sudden
darkening of expression, which made her face
look heavy and dull, turned to follow her from
the room.

Miss Crayston sent a message to Mrs. Armstrong and Miss le Mesurier, and awaited them
anxiously in the office. When they came she
explained the step she had taken, and pointed out
that Nora ought not to suffer for a confession
made under such circumstances. They listened
in silence. Miss Flint joined them, and opened
an attack upon the Lady Resident. She had
heard the address to the students ; a most disastrous and unjustifiable step ; degrading the
ladies of the committee ; offering insults to those

in authority; interfering with those above her. Such were some of the scattered and incoherent phrases with which the Lady Resident was assailed. At length, when Miss Flint's vocabulary was exhausted, the three ladies left the office, and Miss Crayston with a sigh betook herself to her own sitting-room.

Bertie sat with her head between her hands looking up at the clouds :

" Is it all right ? " she asked eagerly.

" I fear not."

Nora Stewart disappeared for a week. At the end of that time she re-appeared, pale, depressed, and sharply watched by Miss Flint, who accompanied her wherever she went. When evening came, and the boarding-house dinner bell sounded, Nora stood at the door of Miss Crayston's room.

" May I come in," she said, " just for a minute ? I'm not going in to dinner. They have told me I may, but I won't ; and they won't miss me from my room, for both the servants are waiting at table."

" Come in, Nora dear : " said Bertie.

Nora walked up to Miss Crayston, and put into her hands a bunch of violets.

" Do have them : " she said ; " I got them

by post.   They grew in my own garden at home."

Miss Crayston rose.   She was agitated.

"Nora," she said, "do you know how sorry I am.   Bertie and I have been more troubled than you can tell.   There is nothing I would not have done for you, Nora; but I am afraid my very efforts made it harder for you."

"Never mind," said Nora, "I don't care a bit for any of them.   Oh, but I do want to go home:" and she broke into a fit of wild, passionate crying.

"Hush, Nora, hush:" said Bertie, "they'll hear you in the next house.   Go back to your room, and leave the window wide open, there's a darling.   You'll see me."

Miss Crayston kissed the girl, tried to console her, and chafed her cold hands; but she also urged her return, and with a rueful look Nora bade them good-bye.

Bertie left the room immediately after, and was absent for half-an-hour.

"I've robbed the larder:" she said on her return.

Miss Crayston looked at her.

"I really have," she continued, "I have taken half a fowl, and some ham, and some cold beef; a lump of seed cake, two rolls, and some butter. I made them into a paper parcel, tied a handkerchief round it, and threw it right into Norah's window at the first shy."

"At what, dear?"

"Oh; you know:"said Bertie, blushing. "The boys call it shying, and I have got into the way of it. Isn't it a good thing I have had so much practice? Well, I put a note in to tell Norah I could see they'd been starving her, and she was to eat what she could and throw the rest out to me."

"Well?" said Miss Crayston, and there was just a shade of constraint in her manner.

"Now don't be angry," exclaimed Bertie. "It was better not to tell you until I had done it; and I'm sure you're very glad that I have done it."

"I really don't know what to say about it, Bertie dear."

"Well, don't say anything. It's of no use now, is it? The thing is done; and Norah wrote that she had had a 'jolly good dinner.' And what do you think she threw back in the handkerchief?" said Bertie, with a merry laugh. "Why the bones of the fowl, and nothing more!"

CHAPTER XII.

AN EVENING PARTY.

WINTER and summer in Minster are alternations of wet and dry, of wind and calm, rather than of cold weather and warm. Snow is rarely seen on the cliffs, and is never known to remain in the city for more than two or three hours, except in those severe winters which may be reckoned by the oldest inhabitant on the fingers of one hand. But the wind is a power almost unknown in more peaceful inland regions. Hurrying across the Atlantic it dashes with horrible force against the granite cliffs, the lofty headlands, and the detached masses of rock which stretch along the north-west coast of Cornwall. The roar of wind and wave is heard continuously for days together, and heavy clouds of sea-spray are drifted inland. The old city of Minster, although it lies in a valley under the shelter of towering cliffs, is not protected from winter

storms ; the streets are not safe for pedestrians
when a gale is raging, and when it is over the
windows of the houses are dull and smeared with
salt sea spray. It is impossible to approach the
sea, so great is the fury of the storm which rages
on it ; and the outer wooden shutters of windows
that face seaward are often closed for weeks
together. It is a perilous exploit to cross the
open market square which lies midway in the
high street, and must be traversed by any one
who would pass from one end of Minster to
the other. At night the gas-lamps are often
extinguished by the fury of the gale, and the old
city is in darkness. But merry groups may be
heard if they are not seen. They cling together
as they are piloted down the less-exposed streets
by some adventurous youth who braves the fury
of the gale and the blinding sleet in his eyes, and
carries a lantern at his back for the guidance of
those who follow. During the college session
Minster offers to its students no lack of interest
and society : there are concerts, lectures, debating
societies, evening parties, and now and then a
dance. Each of the Professors receives students
at least once or twice during the winter, and the
Principal has a monthly re-union, presided over
during the absence of Lady Mary by her cousin

Mrs. Mereweather, the wife of an old Indian general.

At these re-unions the ladies from St. Mary's meet the Minster graduates and under-graduates. Miss Flint is there with grey ringlets and dark eyes, and the peculiar droop of the corners of the mouth, which has earned for her the title of *The Lugubrious*. A few of the boarders accompany her; unhappy-looking girls, who never escape from the watchful care of their supervisor and the depressing effect of her presence. Nora Stewart does not go out. She is not often seen in the class-rooms. It is said that she has a cold, and as Mrs. Armstrong remarks a *temper*. Miss Flint does not encourage inquiries made with regard to her, and rarely allows any one to visit her in the small room where the Irish girl sits with a worn and tired face watching the heavy clouds and the driving rain. The Lady Resident and Bertie are already popular. Some of the youths complain that there is a certain stand-offishness about Bertie, and that they cannot get on with her.

"She is quite right," said Lord Ronald Adair; "they are fellows who ought not to be able to get on with her."

But the greater number of those received by

Principal Ellice gather around the Lady Resident and Miss Ravenshaw as soon as they appear,
telling them of every occurrence likely to interest
them, asking advice on every conceivable subject,
and giving it as freely as they ask.

There was an alarm of fire one night at St.
Mary's, and a room in the boarding-house suffered
considerably. The young men at the next meeting urged Miss Flint to induce all the girls to
form themselves into a volunteer fire-brigade, of
which she should be the captain. Young Carmichael and James Talbot, who were enthusiastic
volunteers in the Minster Brigade, offered to
make all arrangements and ensure due instruc-
tion in the use of hose and bucket and ladder;
but the Lugubrious lifted her sad eyes and said:

"I think you forget that in the boarding-
house we receive only ladies:" and turned away.

The young men walked to a window near
them.

"There it is:" said young Carmichael. "It is
the women themselves who are impracticable.
Why shouldn't they pass a bucket as well as a
man? Why should they all want to stand
screaming at the windows and be burnt to death
because they can't use a ladder or a rope?"

"But," interrupted Lord Ronald, "they don't

all want to do that; and it is not every woman who is afraid of new things."

"No," said James Talbot; "but all the old women are; they are all conservative."

"Old men are equally conservative:" suggested Lord Ronald.

"No doubt:" acquiesced Talbot; "but they can't enforce their conservative notions on younger men, who at any rate get their fling, and move, if it is only an inch forward, before they subside into conservatism."

"That is what makes me sorry for women:" said Carmichael; "they never do get their fling. The old ones are down upon them at once, and they submit and acquiesce. Why shouldn't they have a fire-brigade and a debating club, and lots of other things that everybody seems to think so good for men?"

"Don't you think they are getting a great many things that are good for them?" asked Lord Ronald.

"Not half so many as they deserve," replied the youth gallantly; "and I tell you, when I get into the House I intend regularly to go into every woman's question, and to go in on the woman's side; so do Carmichael and Wills, and a lot of us."

" But I'll tell you another thing : " added Carmichael : " it will be of no use to attempt to help
them so long as girls are led about by a woman
like Miss Flint. Just see : she is taking those
four girls home for fear they should hear us mention the fire-brigade ; and she kept them all in
the house for a month when Adair tried to get
his cousin and Mrs. Mereweather to start a
Debating Club for ladies. And that woman is
considered a treasure !"

" I don't care so much about that : " said Lord
Ronald. " What tries me is, that she is a woman's
rights woman, and if she can get hold of you she
will talk for an hour in a way to make your blood
run cold. She can't see that she is trying to
begin at the wrong end of things."

" It is not so much that : " said Talbot. " She is
the wrong person to begin at any end."

The three young men had turned away and
were talking together.

" Come and tell me about the brigade : " said
the Lady Resident : " Miss Ravenshaw and I
have been saying that we should very much like
to know how much it would be possible for a
woman to do in time of danger."

" Just as much as a man," replied Talbot
eagerly, " and often more ; because I believe that

women are mainly what Goldworthy Fynes would call altruistic, whilst men are mainly egoistic."

" We won't be diverted from the principal issue : " said Bertie. " We want to hear about fire-brigades, and not about altruism."

Now when Miss Flint heard a mention of fire-brigade she had taken alarm, because, knowing the depravity of the masculine mind, she at once concluded that the young men wanted to come up to the house and drill the girls ; but Miss Crayston and Bertie, who had no theories as to masculine or other depravity, had been struck by the suggestion that women might give organised help in time of danger by fire, and so they approached the subject fearlessly.

The young men had really no views of the kind suspected by Miss Flint. They were gentlemen, with sisters of their own, and more disposed to err on the side of excess of chivalrous consideration than the reverse.

They explained the work of volunteers in a fire-brigade with great interest, and soon made it evident that they neither wished nor expected to have anything to do with the drill. Sergeant Roberts, late hero in the Crimea, was, they said, the person into whose hands the matter should be placed.

" You see," said Carmichael, " I know something
of the danger, because my sister Margery was in
the boarding-house for six months whilst my
mother was in Italy. From what she tells me
those twenty girls will be smoked to death like
rats in a hole if a fire breaks out. Now Roberts
has got three daughters, and only the other day
he was telling me that they know what to do in
case of fire as well as he does, and he can rely on
their doing it. I do wish, Miss Crayston, you
would see him."

" We could do nothing without the co-operation of Miss Flint."

" Surely you might make a suggestion to some
member of the committee :" urged Talbot.

" I think that ' rat in a hole ' would be effective :" said Bertie demurely, and they all laughed.

" Miss Ravenshaw, you might start a volunteer
brigade in the College, and then Miss Flint and
the house would be sure to follow :" pleaded Lord
Ronald.

Bertie shook her head, and Miss Crayston
replied that it was for Miss Flint to lead and for
them to follow.

" Miss Crayston," exclaimed a young man who
approached, " I have tried in vain to catch your
eye. You have missed such an awfully jolly fight."

" Who has been fighting ?" asked Bertic.

" Our dear old Doctor Lloyd and that man with the big jaw. I don't know his name. He is a friend of Professor Fynes."

" It is James of London," said young Talbot, " the great anatomist. What have they been saying ? "

" Well, James, if that is his name, has been showing that the construction of the human eye gives proof of great carelessness. There are so many errors on the side, both of excess and defect, that really in hearing him speak I did not merely feel how much better *he* would have done it, I felt I could have made a better eye myself."

There was a general laugh as the speaker, Christopher Horton, a small, spare youth, with a smooth sallow face, large mouth, and mobile features, sat down by the side of the Lady Resident, and picked up her lace shawl which had fallen to the ground.

" The human eye is bad enough : " continued Horton, " but when poor Mr. James began to describe the manner in which the femur of the camel is articulated in the pelvis he was really shocked, almost too shocked to go on. The whole arrangement seems to show such gross and criminal neglect."

"When did Dr. Lloyd intervene:" asked Bertie.

"Oh, he was all about. He said that by common consent the brain and intellect had been given over to the psychologist, but he did think the Almighty might have been trusted to make a bone; in fact, he seemed to think it more presumptuous to criticise a bone than a brain."

"I wish I had heard them:" said Carmichael.

"I wish you had. The Doctor made a splendid shot. He was actually audacious enough to quote a verse of Isaiah in support of one of his statements."

"What effect did it produce?"

"It was just like the bursting of a bombshell. The London man lifted himself off his chair by the hair of his head, and said, 'Is it possible that you adduce that as either proof or argument?' Fynes threw himself back in his superb way as if disgust had almost destroyed him, and said: 'It is useless to carry on a controversy where only one side is represented.'"

"How insolent he is!" exclaimed Bertie with a hot blush. The young men saw the blush and looked angrily at their Professor. Just then they did not consider him at all a distinguished person.

A few words from Bertie or Miss Crayston were enough at any time to give a distinct set and current to their views. In the elder lady the under-graduates recognised a person to be treated with an exceptional degree of confidence and respect. They were not insensible to her beauty; but, quite independent of beauty, she was gifted with that inexplicable personal charm which draws to itself everything that is noble and of good repute. It was this which caused her on all hands to receive moral support; and she was one of those able not only to attract esteem, but to retain it. Principal Ellice and the more earnest among the Professors recognised her as a distinct power in the University, as a person whose influence over the under-graduates was as great and valuable as over the girls at St. Mary's. The Principal looked at Professor Nicholl, and smiled when young Horton withdrew from the group of dons who were listening to the eminent London anatomist, and joined the little group gathered round the Lady Resident.

The same thought was in the minds of both. They were glad that the young men should talk over the new views at that time and in that place.

Bertie also counted for much. She did not

possess the influence which a few years seniority gave the Lady Resident, but she called forth unlimited enthusiasm. Her youth and beauty were alone sufficient to make her popular; and it was also impossible not to see that she was aspiring after a high ideal of human life, and that her aspirations were sustained by warm human sympathy.

Then, too, her nature was docile and trustful. She lived habitually in a condition of elevated feeling, and amongst those who were characterised by nobility of nature, and she lived easily with them. Things that were pure and of good repute were native to her.

The Professors who knew her best and Miss Crayston herself had sometimes been startled by the passionate earnestness which she sometimes showed; but the under-graduates recognised and admired the generous ardour, the courage indomitable, and a strength of conviction equalling their own.

The two ladies did more in a few months to change the set of opinion in Minster with regard to St. Mary's and the higher education of women, than the combined efforts of the council and the University staff had been able to effect in as many years.

They did much to put down the sneering depreciation of high feeling which is not distasteful to the immature mind, since it may be considered as an assumption of superiority; and they were more successful than the most eager advocates of Wordsworth's philosophy in limiting the influence of those exalted few, who had hitherto led the under-graduates, and who scorned to acknowledge that they had any high principles of action at all.

It was not so much anything said or done, it was what they were, that placed Miss Crayston and Bertie in the position they occupied. It was the influence of earnest and beautiful natures which gave to their lives the sweet and pure flavour that acted as an irresistible charm. It was all very well for Mrs. Armstrong, Miss le Mesurier, Miss Ellen Green, Miss Flint, and others of that class, to talk about sex and prerogative, privilege and abuse, to organise public meetings and to advocate repeal of laws and the admission of women to the suffrage. They gathered to themselves those like them, and alienated more than they added.

But the two ladies from St. Mary's, by their very silence and reserve on all topics affecting the respective condition of men and women, by

their gracious confidence in the courtesy and
consideration of all men, carried easily the
position which the others in vain had attempted
to storm. Indeed they did not even carry
the position, the gates were thrown open to
them.

"Why should women be debarred from advanced study and intellectual pursuits?" asked
young Carmichael. "Does it do them any harm?
Just look at Miss Ravenshaw!"

"What paltry stuff it is," said Lord Ronald,
"when you hear people urging that a woman is
incapable of reasoning, and can't follow an argument. I should like them to see the eyes of
the Lady Resident fixed upon you as you speak.
I should like them to find out, as I have often
done, that she detects a fallacy, as it seems,
almost instinctively. She doesn't run at you
with a Saxon halberd, or shoot a great wooden
arrow from a cross-bow, but she pricks you
between the joints with the finest needle, and
you are undone."

And so it came to pass that the whole burden
of the trouble at St. Mary's was taken up and
borne upon masculine shoulders. The Professors
met and discussed pecuniary difficulties and
ways to meet them, and the under-graduates

themselves were a guard of honour to the students of St. Mary's.

"Do you know," Miss Crayston says on this evening, "that one of the under-graduates is giving us some trouble?"

"No!" is the simultaneous exclamation of two young men, whilst two others approach with a sudden look of alert attention.

"Is it worth while to speak of it?" asks Bertie with an appealing look.

"Certainly:" says Lord Ronald with decision; "we may be able to help you."

"I am sure that you will:" replies the Lady Resident, "and I will tell you what it is. A young girl who comes to College, lives a mile on the other side of Minster. An under-graduate watches her, speaks to her, follows her; she arrives breathless and in tears; frightened, and yet without power or courage to put an end to the persecution!"

"What a shame! Who is the fellow!"

"We can't find out. I have sent Gibson, the porter, to meet her or conduct her home, and of course then he has contrived to keep out of the way. I think if he could be told it was unmanly to frighten a girl it would have some effect on him!"

"Yes:" said Talbot, drawing himself up; "I

think if we remonstrate with him we may put a
stop to it."

Talbot was over six feet, and a brawny,
muscular fellow. Bertie, who had brothers,
understood him at once.

She smiled, and yet hesitated :

" My mother says that unless a young lady
behaves as if she was a little milliner she need
fear no annoyance from a gentleman."

"That is a little hard of you, Miss Ravenshaw :" replied Carmichael. " Why should the
little milliner be annoyed ?"

" Of course not," replies Bertie ; " and I think
you ought to interfere on her behalf; but in a
case like this I do think a lady might——"

Bertie blushed and hesitated.

"You are quite right," said Lord Ronald
gravely ; "my sister Joscelyn thinks as you do ;
a *lady* is never insulted."

" But, my dear fellow :" exclaimed Carmichael,
"just imagine any man taking a liberty with
Miss Ravenshaw or Lady Joscelyn Adair."

"That is Miss Ravenshaw's point. I take it
that Miss Crayston, Miss Ravenshaw, and my
sister Joscelyn would be as secure from annoyance in a strange city as here in Minster where
they are known."

"Now you must hear me on behalf of my young friend:" exclaimed Miss Crayston. "She is a delicate, nervous little thing, and has no physical strength, and probably very little presence of mind or courage."

"Is it Millicent Graham?" asked Carmichael.

"It is:" replied Miss Crayston; "but of course you will not repeat it."

"You don't mean to say any fellow is such a cad as to annoy *her!*" exclaimed Horton, starting off his chair. "I say, Adair, we *must* put a stop to it."

"I believe I know who it is:" said Carmichael. "It's that Simon. I have seen him loitering about, with a flower stuck in his button-hole."

"I think," said Lord Ronald, turning to Miss Crayston with a smile, "that we shall be able to persuade him it is not good form to follow a lady."

"Thank you:" replied the Lady Resident.

Bertie rose and went up to Carmichael. She looked him in the eyes and said:

"You'll give him a chance, I suppose?"

"What do you mean?" asked the young man.

"Well," replied Bertie," if he is the man you say, he is such a miserable little creature I think you might make him over to Mr. Horton."

Carmichael laughed and said, "I don't think we need trouble Talbot; but I should like to say a word to him myself. You see I know Miss Graham's people."

As the two ladies were slowly driving home through the wind and storm Bertie said :

"I can't help thinking about that poor Simon."

"Your sympathy is unnecessary. The sense of moral reprobation on the part of young men whose position causes them to be leaders in the University will have more effect on such a delinquent than anything I could do or say."

"They don't intend to argue, or appeal, or to rely upon moral force," replied Bertie; "they'll lick him."

"My dear child!" exclaimed Miss Crayston.

"I know:" laughed Bertie; "but when I saw their eyes and the set of the mouth, I knew from our own boys exactly what was going to happen. They'll catch him, and one of them will beat him. He won't be out for a week."

"My dear Bertie, I can scarcely hear a word you say; this wind is terrible, and it seems as if the horse either won't or can't get up the hill."

"It is of no use to open a window:" said Bertie, "we can neither see nor hear what is going on, and I am sure we couldn't walk in the teeth of this gale. I pin my faith on Cornish horses. I saw that Smith had put two in the carriage."

"We certainly shall be jerked out or thrown over:" exclaimed the Lady Resident. "Don't you think we could walk?"

"I don't believe we could stand:" replied Bertie.

By slow degrees they mounted the hill, and at length the carriage stopped at the door of St. Mary's.

"This is a comfort:" said Bertie, "I haven't a bone that is not shaken out of its socket."

The Lady Resident did not reply. She stood a moment on the pavement.

"You have had help, Smith:" she said. "Who are those at the horses' heads?"

"They'm the young gents, miss. If it hadn't been for they, us might ha' stayed at the bottom of the 'ill all night."

Talbot and Carmichael stepped forward, and took off their hats.

"We ventured to follow the carriage," they explained, "for fear the horses should be troublesome."

"The horses is all right," said the driver; "they go over the hill like a shot, they do; it's this 'ere blasted wind, saving your presence, as is too much for 'em. Lor bless you, we'm dragged and shoved 'em all up this 'ill. I wouldn't take another such a job not for a fiver."

"Who's that behind the carriage?" asked the Lady Resident.

"Oh, that's Adair," replied Talbot; "he and Horton have done a good deal of what Smith calls the shoving."

"Good night, and thank you so much:" came in sweet women's voices from the darkness of the doorway.

"Good night, good night:" was called out of the darkness of the night.

"I thought so:" was the mental ejaculation of Miss Flint, as she peered through the Venetian blinds of a window in the boarding-house; "I thought as much! It's impossible to see anything, but they can't have had *five* coachmen."

CHAPTER XIII.

AFTERNOON TEA.

On the outskirts of Minster there are many pleasant houses, with sunny gardens sloping towards the valley, and within sound of the river Eden, which flows rapidly and rather noisily in this last part of its course. They are occupied by people of sufficient means and leisure to ensure attention to all the little details that make house and garden attractive, and no prettier picture of a small English home in a country town can be desired than that formed by Tregarven House.

The drawing-room is somewhat low, but large and irregular. There are handsome old-fashioned tables, chairs, and carved book-cases in it; faded pieces of fine tapestry and exquisite specimens of old china; the scent of dried rose-leaves and spices pervade the room; in a small window at one end of it stands the cage of a squirrel, the poor little beast is incess-

antly at work, and the whirr of his circular cage
is never silent.   This room faces the south-west,
and a broad wooden balcony stretches outside a
window of such large dimensions that it seems
to occupy the entire side of the room.   The
balcony really forms a summer sitting-room, for
it has- a roof and side walls of painted wood,
which provide both privacy and shelter.   Roses,
jasmine, and westeria cover it on the outside,
great bunches of blossom and long wreaths hang
down over the open front; but within, the flowers
are arranged in a more orderly manner.   There
are trees of fuchsia in large tubs, and tall
oleanders with their exquisite bunches of pink
flowers, and glowing scarlet buds.   Hydrangeas,
pink and blue, great masses of colour, fill in
every available space, and spreading tufts of
deep blue lobelia are suspended in wire baskets
from the roof.   A broad flight of iron steps leads
to the garden, which is a long and formal slip of
ground, but redeemed from insignificance by the
care bestowed upon it, and the perfection of its
flowers.   The scent of roses and mignonette fills
the air, and the flower-beds, brilliant with colour,
can be seen in the interstices of the wooden
balustrade.

The window is open, and within the room, on a

low chair placed near a small table covered with
crimson velvet, which age has softened to a tone
rich and luminous, sits the owner of the house,
Miss Ellen Green.

Her friend, Mrs. Armstrong, is seated near
her, on a sofa behind a large table, on which
she has spread out the papers contained in her
bag.

Miss le Mesurier, erect on an ordinary chair,
faces the squirrel, which seems to possess an
occult attraction for her; whilst in an arm-chair
placed opposite the open window, and in full
view of the pretty balcony, its flowers, and the
garden beyond, is Professor Goldworthy Fynes.
His hat is on the floor between his feet, and he
leans forward as he talks, and looks into the
crown of it.

The Professor was a favourite with the managing ladies. He was a man of good family,
possessed some private means, and, when he first
came to England and to Minster, was believed to
be that extremely eligible bachelor, a marrying
man. He paid marked attention to several ladies,
and amongst others to Miss Ellen Green; she
was fifteen years his senior, it is true, but then
her falling off in personal charm had been more
than compensated by increased pecuniary attrac-

tions. Miss Ellen Green and Professor Fynes
sat together, walked and talked together, until
friends began to smile when their names were
mentioned. Miss Ellen Green's conversation
also took a peculiar turn. She seemed to remember all her dear friends who had married
men much younger than themselves, and whose
lives had without exception been prosperous and
happy. Indeed, domestic felicity, according to
her view at this time, could only be secured by a
man's union with a woman who had outlived
the foolish period of early youth, and was able to
advise and control him.

Suddenly Professor Fynes disappeared from
Minster for two years, and on his return he was
found to be engrossed by positivism and indifferent to woman. But with the advent of the
Lady Resident, Miss Ellen Green noted a re-
currence of the old symptoms. Once again the
Professor went about with a book under his arm
and a manuscript in his pocket; it is true that
the book was a volume of Comte, and the manuscript a translation, the merits of which he sought
an opportunity of discussing with the Lady
Resident. Miss Ellen Green was loth to lose the
Professor. She endeavoured to retain him as
friend and ally, and insisted upon consulting him

and obtaining his advice. Her friends were not
unwilling to comply with her wishes, and the
increasing college difficulties made Professor
Fynes a frequent visitor at Tregarven. On this
day he had been asked to give an opinion with
regard to inspection and examination, which the
managing ladies wished to establish in the
college.

"You should make something more like a
scheme:" he says, in reply to a remark of Miss
Ellen Green's. "It is easily done by stating
definitely what classes you propose should be
examined, by what examiners, and within what
time."

"I don't see," replies Mrs. Armstrong, "how
we can do that. Our plans are not sufficiently
matured."

"You will have to do it," he continues with
some asperity, "before any arrangement can be
made; and you may as well do it now to give
your suggestion the air of a scheme."

"What do you think of putting most of the
examinations into the hands of one Professor?"
asks Miss le Mesurier, turning from the squirrel
with a suspicious glance at Mr. Fynes.

"There must be several who could do most of
it:" he replies coldly. "Mr. Nicholl, for ex-

ample, takes pupils in almost every subject of knowledge. He could at all events take logic, history, and mathematics. Such an examiner would be much more competent to report than a stranger; and, if I understand your object, it is to obtain a reliable account of the condition of all the classes at St. Mary's."

"Yes," said Miss Ellen Green, to whom he had more especially appealed. "Yes, of course, that is our object."

"One of them, at any rate:" added Mrs. Armstrong.

"Well, your plan will be less than is expected if it is not more detailed."

"What is the opinion of the Professors with regard to a permanent inspector:" asks Mrs. Armstrong, who has been consulting a letter.

"They will never submit to it, and you may as well give up the idea at once."

"I am not at all sure of that," replies the lady.

"I suppose you will allow," he adds in a hard and rather bitter tone, "that any one who feels himself able to refuse inspection, and takes his stand on his character and reputation, is certainly entitled to do so."

"I think the refusal will be very much misunderstood."

" That will be a matter of perfect indifference to the Professors; but we shall certainly not relinquish the duty of examining our own classes in the college and determining the scholarships."

" Then I don't understand your meaning : " exclaims Miss Ellen Green. " What did you say the Professors would agree to ? "

" I have no desire to say anything that can be considered either binding or final. I think the Professors may be inclined to arrange either for examining one another's classes (as a concession to your wishes), or for the appointment of an examiner from without."

" The first is a very childish suggestion," said Miss le Mesurier tartly; " the last might meet our views."

" I will read what Miss Kimberley Finch says about the appointment of an examiner."

" You need not give yourself the trouble to do so : " interposes the Professor. " I am quite sure nothing will satisfy that lady but her own cut-and-dried method, which we shall certainly not adopt."

" It is a question for the decision of the council," continues Mrs. Armstrong; " and we shall endeavour to make our views prevail there."

" In your place I should do the same, and I

should influence every one to whom I had access : " replies the Professor ; " at the same time I think we can carry our scheme. It may not be all that you want, but it is too fair to be rejected."

" The fact is," says Miss le Mesurier, rising from her chair to draw nearer to the speakers, " we are quite resolved to secure means of testing the teaching of the Professors, and we intend to do it in the way that seems best to ourselves, for it is of no use to make the cook a judge of the pudding."

" And we," replied the Professor, also rising, " are equally resolved, that if any examiner is appointed he shall be nominated by the Professors. We will not consent to leave the nomination to the ladies. And we are moreover prepared to show that the payment of such examiners cannot be borne by the income of the college."

Miss Ellen Green, who was deeply troubled at what threatened to be a complete rupture between the managing ladies and the only Professor on whom they could rely, burst into tears. Mr. Fynes was angry with her for crying, and also angry because he had been goaded into saying more than he had intended. He looked at her with some contempt and said :

"You should not take things so much to heart. In my own affairs I always make up my mind to fight for the ground inch by inch, and allow it to be seen that such is my intention. In that way I never feel annoyed at anything that happens."

He left the room, and Mrs. Armstrong coming forward, whispered: "What a French monkey he looks with his flaming black eyes! I hate to see a man sit and shrug his shoulders in that supercilious way! Did you see the flower in his button-hole? He is going to Mrs. Brownlow's. The Lady Resident will be there. He will tell her everything that has taken place here."

"There is nothing to tell:" said Miss le Mesurier.

Miss Ellen Green dried her eyes: "I think we ought to try and keep one ally among the Professors. Two years ago they were all on our side, and ready to do anything we asked; and now, if it was not for Fynes we should not even know their plans."

The three ladies when they were together always spoke of the Professors as Brownlow, Fynes, Nicholl, Walmsley, and so on. It was a custom they had adopted from Miss Kimberley Finch, who used the same form in her letters.

"I don't see what we are to do!" continued Miss Ellen Green.

"Carry out your own suggestion," urged Mrs. Armstrong, "and ask Miss Kimberley Finch to pay you a visit. Let her see things with her own eyes. Her advice will be far more valuable if she has a full knowledge of the whole affair. I shall write an account of this interview, and perhaps you will feel disposed to add a note of invitation. Did you say, Barbara, that you were going to the Brownlows'?"

"Yes:" replied Miss le Mesurier. "Some one ought to go. All Minster will be there, and it will look strange if we stay away."

"Perhaps we may look in, later on, when these letters are finished:" said Mrs. Armstrong. "Fynes always remains to the last, so that we shall meet him again."

"I wonder if he would like Miss Kimberley Finch to come:" says Miss Ellen. "I don't think it prudent to annoy him."

Distance does not count for much as an element affecting intercourse in Minster; and Mrs. Armstrong retraced her steps to the old city, and passing through it, began the ascent toward St. Mary's. The road slopes gently upwards for half a mile before you reach the College, but the

row of houses called the Parade, two of which
are occupied by Mr. Brownlow and Mr. Nicholl,
is not more than seven minutes' walk out of
Minster.   Miss le Mesurier found the front door
open at Mrs. Brownlow's, as usual on days of
high festivity; for the two maids in their neat
caps, faultless white aprons, and brown serge
gowns, were busy with the tea and the guests.
She entered what had been the dining-room, but
was now the Professor's study, in which tea was
laid out on a long table, together with piled-
up plates of strawberries and great jugs of
cream.

"We draw our commissariat supplies from this
source:" said the Professor, who advanced to
meet Miss le Mesurier; "but I think you will find
it pleasanter in the garden.   Mrs. Brownlow is
there, and if you will allow me I will bring you
out some strawberries and cream."

"Thank you, I never take them."

"Shall I give you a cup of tea?"

"If you please.   No sugar."

"How very pretty this room is!" exclaimed
Miss Graham, who entered with Miss le Mesurier.
"I think the gilding just above the black shelves
is perfect.   I suppose you intend it to frame
your beloved books like a picture, Mr. Brownlow,

and your wall-paper is quite ideal. You must have had that down from London."

"Yes:" replied the Professor, well pleased. "It is my wife's choice. In fact the arrangement of the room and books is her own ; and she has crowned her good deeds by writing out a catalogue with illustrations:" he added, with a smile. "She would not approve of my showing them to an artist, but I should really like to know what you think of her sketches."

"Oh, charming!" exclaimed Miss Graham, a kindly and appreciative creature, who looked out for something to praise in all that she saw. "What a pretty title-page. Those wild flowers are perfect, and the Cupid down among the water-lilies is most suggestive."

"I can't see the wings," said Miss le Mesurier, "nor any legs or feet."

"Ah, I am afraid you have hit upon the weak spot, Miss le Mesurier. I rather fancy my wife intends that figure for the baby. It is a mere suggestion ; she is self-taught. Perhaps I ought not to have shown her work."

"Indeed, you ought to be proud of it. I never saw prettier marginal sketches, nor more graceful fancy in minute details:" replies Miss Graham.

The Professor looked proud and pleased, and turned to Miss le Mesurier, who was examining the book-shelves with an air of dissatisfaction.

"I think you don't quite approve of them?" he asked.

"Well," she said, "I suppose it is a new fashion; and you see I am not accustomed to black out of an undertaker's shop."

"Shall we join my wife?" suggests Mr. Brownlow, turning sharply to Miss Graham.

They passed through the little dining-room, descending steps leading from the window to an old-fashioned garden, or rather to the gardens of the two houses thrown into one. There was a large and carefully-kept lawn, with a croquet ground on the most level part of it. Croquet was played under difficulties on account of the slope of the ground; but this was a condition incidental to all Minster gardens, and, as Mr. Brownlow said, merely required to be taken into account by the players. Round the lawn were shaded walks, lovers' walks Mrs. Brownlow called them; and beyond the lawn was the wilderness, a bit of wild, uncultivated land, where brambles and dog-roses grew amongst hazel trees and young oaks, where birds built in safety, and from whence the song of the thrush was always heard in spring. Narrow paths intersected the wilderness; the children played there. They watched for the nests of the finches, the robins, and the thrushes; carried crumbs and biscuits for the old birds, counted their eggs, and fiercely chased any cat that appeared in the vicinity.

On this day three of the little Nicholls were on their way through the wilderness. The nurse and a younger child had preceded them, and they were close to a gate of egress, by means of which they passed to a space of broken open ground, covered with gorse and heather, and leading upward to the park at the summit of the cliff. Each child wheeled a barrow, of size suited to its age, and at the gate they met Bertie. She waited for them to pass through, and when they had done so, and arranged their barrows side by side, they turned round and lifted three pairs of eyes to her face.

"Well, darlings:" said Bertie. "Nurse and baby are not far off. You will see the perambulator when you pass the thorn tree."

The children looked at each other in silence. They let go the handles; each child retreated and sat down on a little wooden ledge in front of the barrow; then the youngest, a boy of three years old, fixing his eyes on Bertie, said slowly:

" Baby is dead.   His name is Archie."

" He has gone to the happy angels : " added little Maud, who was four.

" He is away, away, to a far, far happier place : " chanted Grace, a girl of five years old ; and then they all looked steadfastly at Bertie.

" Yes, darlings ; I know that the blessed Jesus has taken baby, but I did not mean him.   I met nurse with little Bell, and I thought perhaps you call her baby now."

" She isn't baby : " replied Grace, very earnestly. " Her name is Bella."

" It is Auntie Bell," stated Maud, with pre-cision, " and sister Bella."

" Baby is dead," chimed in little Willie, " and his name is Archie."

" And where is Ralph ? " asked Bertie, by way of changing the conversation.

" Mamma said he might stay with her because it is his birthday : " answered Grace.

" He is seven, and aunty has gave him a box of croquet : " said Maud.

At this point they all executed a dance round the barrows, and exclaimed together : " He says we shall play to-morrow."

Bertie passed on and joined the party in the garden.   Miss Crayston had preceded her, and was sitting on a garden seat under a group of laburnum trees. Professor Fynes was standing by her side.

"I should like to put in a clear light some remarks of mine in our last conversation, which I think you found rather startling:" he said.

"You spoke of religion being an encumbrance to morality:" she replied, "from which I conclude you to mean that a sincerely religious person will find morality more difficult."

"I mean nothing of the kind; but it occurred to me afterwards that you might think so. I hold religion, as I said in my lecture, to be indispensable to the happiness of the individual and the progress of the race."

"Yes; I remember that you said so, and it seems to me difficult to reconcile that statement with your present assertion, that unless a man disbelieves he will be immoral."

"When did I say that?" asked the Professor, angrily. "On the contrary, I say (a general proposition about individuals being liable to unascertainable exceptions), that if society does not believe some religion its morality will decline."

"Well, society does believe *some* religion, and you say that its religion is an encumbrance to its morality!"

"Modern society," urged the Professor with some warmth, "is unable to believe the religions that suited our fathers, and I think it is high time some religion was found that does not outrage the intellect. Tyrolese peasants, who are really devout Catholics, and believe everything, may get along very well at present as they are; but for us some new provision is indispensable."

"I object to the term *outrage the intellect:*" replied Miss Crayston. "Men of the highest intellectual power in the present day are also devout Christians."

"I know there are many of such who profess Christianity. They are all wretched hypocrites. In fact, English ladies don't know how utterly their husbands and brothers have ceased to believe."

"And what do you expect to gain if you offer them a new superstition?"

"Whatever Positivism is, it is not a superstition:" he warmly replied. "It discards the supernatural, and asks assent to nothing which human reason cannot understand. It is eminently practical. It seeks the happiness of the individual, and the progress of the race."

"So does Christianity:" said Miss Crayston.

"It embraces much more, but it also includes individual well-being and human progress."

"Not at all :" replied the Professor. "*Christians*," and he emphasised the word in a contemptuous manner, "speak of religion, but they mean theology and dogma. Now-a-days, if people are habituated to couple together the Divinity of Jesus and moral duty as facts of equal certainty, it will go hard with the latter."

"I think you had better give me your definition of religion :" said Miss Crayston. "I feel very much as if you were describing a corporeal entity, and forbidding me to think of the skin and the muscle and the bones.

"I take religion to be the systematic effort to develop the social or unselfish feelings, and to discipline the selfish with a view to unity."

"Yes. I know that in a simpler form. Thou shalt love thy neighbour as thyself."

"Of course. All founders of religion have arrived at it : Moses, Mahomet, St. Paul, Confucius, even Brigham Young I am disposed to think, though I should like to look into his social system and its workings a little more carefully before speaking confidently—— "

"Bertie, dear," said Miss Crayston to that young lady who had approached and was about

to take a seat by her side.   "I think Mrs.
Brownlow wants you.   I told her I was sure
you would give Ralph Nicholl his first lesson in
croquet."

Bertie gave a glance which meant : "May I
stay with you ?" but Miss Crayston replied :
"You will find him somewhere on the lawn :" and
when Bertie had retreated she looked up at Mr.
Fynes, and said :

"And after that ?"

"Well," he resumed, with a rather bitter smile,
as he watched Bertie cross the lawn, and recognised the fact that she had been sent away,
"all these systems have adopted and taken into
alliance some base part of our nature to control
better by its help the rest.   Thus Christianity
addresses itself to our cowardice."

"Don't you think," interrupted Miss Crayston
with some warmth, "that you had better also
look into that a little more carefully before speaking confidently ? "

The Professor smiled ; he had a lofty sense or
his own superiority in the argument.

"I grant you," he continued, "that the object
of Catholicism, of course I include Protestantism
in Catholicism, the object of Catholicism in its
best times was not to save men's souls from hell-

fire, but to improve human society; and this original aim is not entirely obliterated."

"I am glad you concede so much; but I presume you consider those good times at an end?"

"Decidedly. Catholicism is now in its decline, it has lost sight of the real end of religion, and made theology its serious business."

"And you think that Positivism can supply all that Christianity lacks?"

"I was not speaking of Christianity. I know nothing about it. It is not a religion, it is a collection of rags and tatters, not worthy of investigation; but I state confidently that Positivism is distinguished from all other religions by appealing exclusively to the highest and purest parts of our nature."

"How can you speak of Positivism as a religion?" said Miss Crayston. "There can be no religion without a God!"

"I beg your pardon. Religion may exist without a belief in God; and John Stuart Mill holds that M. Comte is fully justified in the attempt to develop his philosophy into a religion, and that he has realised the essential conditions of one."

Miss Crayston looked puzzled and somewhat pained; and the Professor, who was not anxious to close the conversation, considered that he had made a notable concession when he added:

"Positivism is not, to my own mind, incompatible with Theism, though perhaps complete Positivists would say that the introduction of a God is purely mischievous. For my own part I think if we will pry into first causes a God is the easiest hypothesis; but I don't see how I am to know much about him, or what my relations to him are. So much seems clear, that doing my duty to humanity must be my best way of serving him, which dispenses me from looking further than humanity."

"Then you also dispense with any necessity for worship or prayer. You strip your life bare to the very bones, and yet find it possible to hold it up for admiration and imitation."

"We do nothing of the kind. The Positivist religion makes provision for both worship and prayer."

"Worship of what?"

"The worship of woman, who is the representative of humanity."

"That seems to me very shocking. 'Thou shalt worship the Lord thy God, and Him only shalt thou serve.'"

"It is not shocking at all; and you employ a

very feminine mode of argument. But I allow
that it is perhaps impossible for those who have
been brought up as Protestants to realise com-
pletely the Positivist worship of humanity, and
of woman as its representative."

"Most assuredly it is:" said Miss Crayston,
with a smile, "especially if I am to accept your
own definition of worship. Don't you remember
that in our previous conversation you 'defied' me
to define worship otherwise than as 'the service
of an Omnipotent Being, with whom we have
nothing in common?' Now I place the ideal
woman on a lofty pedestal, but I do not hold her
to be omnipotent, or——"

"I said," interrupted the Professor, angrily,
"that that was the English idea of worship. Of
course it would be an abuse of terms to apply it
as Comte does. We are slaves to a word. But
I imagine a Catholic, accustomed from infancy to
the admirable institution of Mariolatry, has no
such difficulty, because *worship* with him has a
much broader and more practical significance."

"I thought you told me you had been brought
up as a Protestant."

"Yes. And I can say from my own experi-
ence, that it is very difficult at first even to grasp
the idea of humanity in a Positivist sense."

" Have you overcome that difficulty ? "

" Certainly.   By steadily habituating my mind
to contemplate it, I do grasp it now ; and I think
I can realise what Comte meant by worship of it,
namely, gratitude, love, and devotion to it."

" Do you speak now of humanity, or of woman
as its representative ? "

" Oh, of humanity.   I thoroughly share Comte's
views as to the function and influence of women ;
but I confess I do not so clearly apprehend his
meaning when he puts her as a type of humanity ;
nor do I see what the worship of her amounts
to when figurative and metaphorical language is
stripped away.   I believe my difficulties on this
point are shared by English Positivists, and by
all thinking people of my own sex."

" I am quite prepared to expect that : " replied
Miss Crayston, coldly ; " and now that you have
explained the worship of woman, I should very
much like to know what I am to understand by
prayer."

" I imagine prayer to mean meditation on a
type and aspiration ; and I suppose most thinking people have a repugnance to give any other
character to their prayer."

" Well, then, I must say that most thinking
people get nothing out of their worship, and very

little out of their prayer, and I should eliminate
those two elements from the Positivist religion."

" But you can't eliminate them," exclaimed the
Professor, " from humanity."

" Mr. Fynes," said Mrs. Brownlow, who had
approached, " you have talked humanity with a
capital H under this tree for an hour, and I
am going to take Miss Crayston away. Mr.
Walmsley has been looking pensive and quoting:

    ' Laburnums, dropping wells of fire.' "

" I should imagine he is disappointed at not
seeing a fender under the trees:" Miss Crayston replied ; and the two ladies laughed as they recalled
Mr. Walmsley's well-known seat in every room.
Mr. Fynes did not laugh, he made no reply, but
walked away in silence.

" What have you been talking about for so
long ? "

" Positivism.   It is a subject that has caused
a complete separation between me and a very
dear friend, and I want to understand more
about it."

" Well, do you know I am very glad you had
Mr. Fynes here in the open. Mr. Nicholl met
him at the Jacksons' the other night, and from
what I can understand he talked blasphemy

enough to blow the roof off. Now don't laugh, because his views are a real calamity in a place like this."

"But he makes no secret of them. They must have been well known when he was elected."

"Oh, don't you see that he has all the ardour of a fresh convert. He went away for two years on account of his health, and when. he came back he had got a new religion. He is a terrible kind of man, and not at all original. These Positivists reproduce the old savage period, so John says."

"In what way?" asked the Lady Resident.

"John thinks that a Positivist goes about after a woman he admires with an intellectual cudgel, and when he has beaten her senseless he expects her to consent to marry him. But we won't stay to talk about Goldworthy Fynes. I want to introduce Philip le Mesurier to you. He is rather a fine fellow in his way, and we are all fond of him. I never understand a word he says; you musn't try to make sense out of his utterances, but just let them wash over you like a sea wave, and you'll feel all the better for it. I left him under a tree gazing at Bertie."

CHAPTER XIV.

MATCH MAKING.

MR. NICHOLL advanced to meet the two ladies, saying :

" I am very glad to see you, Miss Crayston ; Lady Mary is asking for you, and I should like to have the pleasure of introducing you to her."

" I did not know that she had returned to Minster, much less that she was here."

" That was just what I was going to tell you," exclaimed Mrs. Brownlow, " but the laburnum tree put it out of my head."

" Mrs. Brownlow's garden party," said Mr. Nicholl, " is, as usual, a great success. It is *the* event of the year. Lady Mary arrived last evening, and no doubt she returned expressly for it. She looks extremely delicate, and I fear has not gained so much as we had hoped from change of climate. Some star always follows in her luminous track, and this year she has brought Mr. Otto Venning."

" The poet ? "

" Yes. There he is in a shawl. You may perhaps have noticed that a poet always wears a shawl."

" Mr. Nicholl, I shall leave Miss Crayston in your charge, for there are. so many fresh arrivals that I must not stay with you."

" I will conduct her to Lady Mary as soon as I see an opportunity. Just now there is no possibility of doing so."

Mr. Nicholl was the Professor of History at Minster, and he held a class on that subject at St. Mary's. He was a man rather beneath the middle height, active, vigorous, energetic, with dark hair, ruddy complexion, and black eyes glancing keenly through spectacles. He was popular with all the best students, for his enthusiasm gave an intense reality to all his own work and to theirs also.

" Miss Crayston, why don't you send Miss Ravenshaw to me ? " he asked ; " the Principal says she is the most promising pupil he ever had, male or female. Walmsley raves about her, and even Fynes confesses that a woman under twenty may have something that approaches the nature of Intellect."

" I think you ought to talk to her yourself,

Mr. Nicholl; she says that history is too great
for her. Just at present she works so hard that
I don't see how she could take on another subject
of study."

"Oh, I wasn't in earnest. But I think I shall
say she must come to me next session. My wife
brings home the most wonderful accounts of her.
Don't let her do too much. Look; do you see
that grey-haired man playing with my boy Ralph.
That is Dobson, the charity organisation man.
I suppose he came down with le Mesurier."

"What do you think of charity organisation?"

"An excellent thing; but the name is a mistake.
It is all organisation and no charity. See, there's
Lady Mary on that low couch under the trees.
What do you think of *her*?"

"She is very beautiful; and how young she
looks."

"She always produces the impression of beauty,
and always will, though she is no longer young,"
said Mr. Nicholl. "When Villars, the sculptor,
was here some years ago, he said a thing I thought
very true. He said she was not the most beautiful woman he had ever known, but that he had
seen her look more beautiful than any other
woman."

"She looks at once sensitive and sympathetic."

" She is so," replied Mr. Nicholl. " At the same time her critical judgment is very good. It is quick and penetrating."

" That is a rare combination in a woman."

" It is," said Mr. Nicholl. " I have known women as full of sensibility and imaginative atmosphere as Lady Mary, but none in whom intellect made such exigent demands, and in whom there was so much reserve of that which constitutes the charm of her character."

" It is a pleasure to stand and watch her : " said Miss Crayston.

" Yes ; for you see how the observant mind controls her warm social impulses. See, she notices us. That is Otto Venning by her side."

They drew near to Lady Mary, and at the same time Mr. Fynes approached and bowed over her hand with his smile of self-satisfaction. She said a few words, and then turned her head towards the poet, who continued to talk. He was a man of four or five-and-twenty, with long fair hair, delicate complexion and blue eyes.

" The fact is," he said, " that the longer I live, and the more I study human nature, the more I perceive that all feminine literature is a mistake."

" Not only a mistake," struck in Mr. Fynes ; " it is an anomaly."

" It seems to be a necessary anomaly just at
present : " smiled Lady Mary.

" That may be : " replied the poet ; " but we
must always, and under all circumstances, recognise feminine literature *as* an anomaly, and
never suffer it to enter into our ideal of human
society."

" You have not outgrown St. Paul : " said Mr.
Nicholl. " I suffer not a woman to speak in the
church."

" Ah, yes," Lady Mary exclaimed. " She is
banished also from the assembly of saints."

" All religious and philosophical teachers, in-
cluding St. Paul," said Mr. Fynes in a hard, dogmatic tone, " are unanimous on this point. It
only remains for us to show that this exclusion
from all participation in active life and intellectual exercise is not derogatory."

" On the contrary," exclaimed Otto Venning
eagerly ; " it is in the highest and divinest degree
honourable to womanhood."

" Mr. Venning, allow me to introduce you to
Professor Goldworthy Fynes : " said Lady Mary.

The two men shook hands warmly, and Mr.
Venning turned to speak to Mrs. Brownlow.

" I have no doubt, Fynes, you have read Mr.
Venning's poems. His *Bethany, St. John of Pat-*

mos, the *Sisters of Lazarus,* and *St. Peter,* are allowed, as you may have heard, to represent the most orthodox views, and at the same time to possess all the characteristics of original genius :" said Mr. Nicholl, and smiled.

" I do not read religious poetry :" replied Mr. Fynes, with a cold, angry stare, and he turned away.

Mr. Venning had drawn the shawl round him, and was gazing at Miss Crayston.

" Who is Goldworthy Fynes ?" he asked.

" Our Positivist :" replied Mr. Nicholl. The poet shuddered.

" For shame, Mr. Nicholl ! you are full of mischief :" said Lady Mary ; " but I must forgive you, since you bring Miss Crayston to me."

" Lady Mary," whispered Mrs. Brownlow, leaning over the couch and speaking low, " can you spare me the poet ?"

" Certainly."

" And may I bring the boy to you presently ? He was fifteen months old yesterday."

" I must look at him to-day ; but you must send him to me for an hour in the morning, or, better still, bring him with you."

" Thanks. Just now I shall keep every one

away, that you may have five minutes' talk with Miss Crayston."

Whilst the two ladies were talking, a man, hat in hand, stood under the trees at no great distance from them, and watched the numerous visitors who now thronged the garden. He was tall, and of a large, heavy build, with enormous hands and feet. His light scanty hair was parted down the middle, and combed straight and even on each side of his head. A fringe of short stubby beard grew beneath his chin, and delineated the form of a lower jaw of portentous mass. Light grey eyes peered mildly through gold-rimmed spectacles. The whole aspect of the man was peaceable, and yet you could not look at him without recognising the prevailing characteristic as one of aggression.

After a time Lady Mary beckoned to him.

"What are you doing under the trees, Mr. Philip?"

"Keeping out of the way of science:" he replied. "Do you see that fellow making love to a most beautiful girl. What does he mean by it? He looks upon himself as descended from a skulking aborigenes; he is spouse of the worm and brother of the clay; he is ready to distil himself into gas or pound himself into cells."

" Oh spare us : " said Lady Mary. " We don't hold with him, do we, Miss Crayston ? "

" He is probably asking her to share his future with him," pursued the speaker ; " his *future state.* Why, according to his own belief it is so much dirty water, a certain proportion of fœtid oil, and so many ounces of scientific dust."

" I don't think he would define his future with quite such precision : " said Miss Crayston, showing slight signs of disgust.

" Do not be too hard upon the sceptics, Mr. Philip : " said Lady Mary. " They have a right to their own time for doubting. God gives them leisure, and I do not see why man should hurry them."

" Just so. So long as they doubt and inquire I have nothing to say. It is their loud-tongued vociferation that there is nothing, because they can see nothing, that I resent."

" Le Mesurier, you are the very man I want : " said the Principal, advancing. " I told my wife you had a new theory of apparitions, and she wishes to know what it is."

" Yes," exclaimed Lady Mary ; " I can't tell which is the most difficult, to believe in apparitions or to disbelieve in them."

" Just so. But I think you hold with me,

that nature is the drapery of spirit; and in that case it must be possible sometimes to come upon spirit unclothed."

"Do you, then," asked Miss Crayston, "look upon an apparition, a ghost, as spirit unclothed?"

"Well, no: that is not exactly my meaning. I think Principal Ellice alludes to a conversation we had respecting the physiological re-appearance of the soul in nature. I was telling him that I hold it to be due to imperfect death."

Miss Crayston looked surprised, and the speaker continued:

"I mean by imperfect death a death after which the proper spiritual changes have not occurred."

"Philip," exclaimed a rough, discordant voice, "what a strange thing for you to be here! I did not know you were in Minster!

"How do you do, Barbara?" said Mr. Philip, making no reply to his sister's ejaculation. "I met Miss Kimberley Finch at Oxford last week, and she gave me a message for you."

They walked away together; and Lady Mary, looking after them, said to Miss Crayston with a smile:

"I never knew brother and sister so unlike each other."

" Is that Miss le Mesurier's brother ? "

" Yes ; that is Mr. Philip, as we all call him
in Minster. You don't know what a good fellow
he is ; and it may take you some little time to
discover it."

" I will tell you what you will find out with
very little trouble, Miss Crayston : " said Mr.
Nicholl. " He is one of those very advanced
thinkers of the present time who condemn
everything, hope for little, and do nothing. I
have known le Mesurier for the last fifteen
years, and I never heard him speak with approval of any existing institution, political,
moral, or religious."

" He looks like an iconoclast : " suggested Miss
Crayston.

" You are right : " said Lady Mary. " He goes
about breaking dolls' heads to see if there is anything in them."

" He has the appearance of a man of action,"
continued Miss Crayston, " or at any rate of a
man who ought to be a powerful speaker."

" The strong aggressive jaw is very suggestive : " assented Lady Mary ; " and I believe he
might, under favourable circumstances, have been
a powerful auxiliary in some good cause."

" I think not : " urged Mr. Nicholl. " He is full

of contradictions and crotchets. Destruction is his element. He might have helped to destroy evil, but not to call forth good; and you will find him far more amusing than instructive.

"And why *might have?*" asked Miss Crayston.

"As a young man he was poor, independent, and ambitious, able to live simply and work hard. In London, whilst he was reading for the bar, a childless uncle and aunt took a great fancy to him, and, dying, left him a considerable fortune. He bought the house in Wimpole St. where he had lodged, and has lived there ever since. He has now abandoned his profession and renounced his creed; and he is original, unintelligible, and visionary."

"You are rather hard upon him:" said Lady Mary. "I think he is in a state of transition, and the outcome of it will be noble action in some direction. Just now he is quite run away with by his search for analogies between the material and spiritual world. He is so intensely honest that everybody respects him, and the suspicion of a craze rather endears him to us all, I think."

"I heard him holding forth to Brownlow upon analogy, which he says is the ' cement of all things and the high road of influence.' "

" The brother and sister are not at all alike in appearance : " said Miss Crayston.

" Nor in character," replied Lady Mary. "She is the eldest and he the youngest of a family of nine children. She is eighteen years older than her brother ; and, although children of the same parents, they seem to have nothing in common. I see," she continued, " what Mr. Philip was doing when he was under that tree ; he was watching that lovely girl in the white serge dress. You need not tell me her name. There can be only one Bertie Ravenshaw in Minster."

Miss Crayston's cheeks glowed with pleasure as she replied :

" Yes ; that is Bertie."

" My husband's letters have made me most anxious to see her, and nothing has given me so much pleasure as to watch her as I have done all this afternoon."

" We are all very proud of her : " said Mr. Nicholl.

" She must have a very happy home, with influences of the best and highest kind ; and I suppose she is one of a large family ? "

" You are right on all points. I think it is the father's character and nature that have exercised so great an influence upon her. She often shows me letters from him, and they attract me more than any I have ever seen. He writes to Bertie with the greatest frankness on all subjects which interest him, and treats her with the tenderness of a father, but also with the respect and consideration due to a companion and friend."

"That enables one to understand the singular charm of her manner with men much older than herself:" said Lady Mary. "That bright blushing face, with the frank eyes and confiding smile, have won my heart. Her whole attitude is one of respectful, I might almost say of affectionate, attention."

"Really that is very pleasant for us:" interposed Mr. Nicholl. "I think I will go and talk to her. Shall I bring her to you, Lady Mary?"

"Any time will do. She is quite as charming with the young men as the old, and please don't bring her away from any one. She is absolutely free from affectation and self-consciousness, and receives their little attentions just in the same way that she would acknowledge the sunshine and the flowers. You are very happy together, are you not?" said Lady Mary, turning to Miss Crayston.

"Very happy."

"And she will return next session?"

"Certainly, so far as I know."

"Lady Mary," said Mr. Brownlow, approaching with Mr. Walmsley, "we have come to ask if you will be well enough to attend the council meeting next week? There will be a few matters of considerable importance which we shall have to decide; as Nicholl is here, perhaps he will tell you our present position."

"Now, pray don't leave us, Miss Crayston," said Mr. Walmsley; "there are no secrets from you."

She bowed and smiled, but walked away.

"My husband tells me," said Lady Mary, "that there is a hitch somewhere; and, in fact, I have really come home sooner than I intended in order to be present at the meeting of the ladies' committee to-morrow, and at the council meeting of next week."

"Then there is no cause for anxiety on any point."

Nevertheless, they remained in conversation for nearly half-an-hour.

During the latter part of that time Miss Ellen Green and Miss Armstrong, who could not very well stay away from an entertainment at which all Minster was present, had arrived. They joined Miss le Mesurier, who greeted them with:

"We may as well give it up at once. My brother tells me Miss Kimberley Finch will stay three weeks longer in Oxford."

"Is that Lady Mary under the trees ?"

"Yes."

"When did she return ?"

"Last evening."

"Then we may certainly as well give it up : " said Miss Armstrong. "We shall not have the slightest chance of carrying our scheme. All the men are against us; they will talk over Lady Mary, and she will influence all the women."

"But Fynes is on our side ?"

"Don't rely upon him : " said Miss le Mesurier. "He will study nothing but his own interest. Just now it will be with that of his colleagues."

"Who is that walking with Miss Ravenshaw ?"

"My brother Philip : " snapped Miss le Mesurier, in a tone which was absolutely prohibitive of further remark.

An hour later Mr. Brownlow said to his wife :

"Well, my dear, I think you must be tired."

"No, really, Jack, I am not. This has been a most festive scene, has it not ? The strawberries and cream have continued to flow through it, and the tea and coffee have never failed. My boy has been petted and kissed to his heart's content, and he will sleep the whole evening, whilst you and I sit and talk it all over."

"And pray when is that to be?" asked the Professor, glancing towards two figures on the lawn.

"Oh, really, John, you must go and put a stop to it. I have tried in vain. Whenever I go near them I hear that extraordinary man holding forth about the motives of separation between the soul and spiritual mind, and the body and natural mind. The last time I passed he looked steadily into my face, shook hands with me, and said something about 'all our relations and utilities having a focal union.'"

"Miss Crayston has now joined them," replied Mr. Brownlow, laughing; "and if she takes Bertie home, le Mesurier will have no one to talk to."

"Tell me what Lady Mary thinks of our Lady Resident."

"She cannot speak warmly enough of her. Miss Crayston has evidently made a most favourable impression, and Lady Mary speaks of the desirability of placing her at the head of a whole college of girl-graduates."

"Oh, Jack! If we could only get rid of Miss Flint! If you could have seen her marshal the six ugliest, worst-drest girls in Minster about

this lawn, and then march them off through the
wilderness, you would have been as angry with
her as I am."

"My love, she is not responsible for their personal appearance, nor, most probably, for their
clothes."

"John, I have often told you that men should
never talk of things they don't understand.　If
Miss Crayston had been in charge of those girls
they would have been well-dressed, good-looking,
and they would have enjoyed themselves."

At this moment Miss Crayston approached.

"We were among the first to come, Mrs.
Brownlow, and you see we are nearly the last to
go.　Bertie and I were saying that it has been one
of our happiest days in Minster, so you can
understand why we are anxious to prolong it."

"Now, Bertie," said Mrs. Brownlow, "you are
to come to-morrow and tell me what you have
been talking about with Mr. Philip.　I always
find when he speaks to me that at the end of
five minutes I have got urgent duties somewhere
else.　I can't understand half that he says, or
anything at all of what he means."

"He *is* difficult:" replied Bertie; "but then,
all he says is so new to me.　I have never thought
about spiritual analogies."

"Bertie!" exclaimed Mrs. Brownlow solemnly, "you are not to begin till you can put it into language I understand. I don't consider you responsible just at present. Miss Graham was only a few minutes with Mr. Philip, and when she left him she came up to me and said something about idiopathic complaints, and the necessity of phrenopathic means of cure. Now, Jack, are there any such words?"

"Yes, my dear; and it does you credit to remember them."

"You must explain them all to-morrow:" Mrs. Brownlow said to Bertie, and the friends took leave of her.

"I have never been more interested in my life:" said Bertie to Miss Crayston. "Do let us go home by way of the wilderness and up over the cliff, and then I shall have time to tell you about it."

"Yes; I am quite willing. It is always delightful to get near the sea; and to-night there will be a sunset, and that vivid emerald light which one sees on the Cornish coast when the sun dips down beneath the waves."

"You must tell me when the time comes to look for it. I am so excited to-night that I shall forget even the emerald gleam."

"What excites you so much, Bertie?"

"If I tell you I know you won't laugh at me, for you never do; and yet I can hardly help laughing at myself. I want Mr. le Mesurier to marry Trissy."

"To marry whom?"

"Trissy. Don't you remember her? Miss Trescott."

"The children's governess?"

"Yes, and ours also; of all us elder ones. She is *so* good and so dear. We all love her. She is not very young, you know, nor very beautiful; but a man like Mr. Philip doesn't care about that, and he would really appreciate her. All that he says about spiritual worth, and beauty, and excellence, and his keen appreciation of them; his hatred of show and appearance, and mere material attractions; all these *convince* me that he and Trissy are really intended for each other. I don't see how it can be managed; but we really must bring them together."

She caught Miss Crayston's hands in her excitement and kissed her.

"Now, isn't it really a good plan?" she asked.

"I don't know," replied the Lady Resident. "I don't at all think that your expectations would be realised."

CHAPTER XV.

POOR NORA.

THE arrival of Philip le Mesurier was usually the signal for the commencement of summer festivities. But this year, after a late and boisterous spring, came a summer wet and cold.

Mrs. Brownlow's garden party was the only one held out of doors; all the others degenerated into tea and talk. Picnics and drives were almost impossible; boating was a failure.

Lady Mary Ellice was compelled to seek a warmer and drier climate. In consequence of her intervention and influence the College difficulties had seemed to vanish. The managing ladies brought forward no schemes; the Professors made no complaints; all dangerous topics were avoided. Mrs. Brownlow said that they had wriggled, and Professor Fynes that they had shuffled, through the meeting; whilst Miss le Mesurier sniffed loudly and said nothing. How-

ever, when the excitement connected with it had
subsided, Lady Mary left Minster, and Mrs.
Milner also left to pay a long-promised visit to a
sister in Normandy.

There was apparent peace ; but those members
of the council who looked beneath the surface saw
that a crisis was approaching which could not
be long averted. The managing ladies were
smarting under a sense of injustice and ingrati-
tude. An institution sheltered in their house,
and supported, as they said, by their money,
refused them any allegiance. They had, in de-
ference to the advice given by Lady Mary, with-
drawn their proposals. Miss le Mesurier, it is
true, had ventured to assert that Miss Flint
ought to be at the head of the College as well as
the house ; but when Lady Mary heard it she
shook her head and laughed ; very sweetly and
gently, it is true, but still she laughed ; and
when she did this the other ladies did not say a
word in support of their friend's suggestion.

For some months the managing ladies had
been endeavouring to show the superiority of
Miss Flint and the house, to Miss Crayston and
the College, and had failed. They were not of
those who can pass through the valley of humi-
liation and learn there the lessons it is intended

to teach. They fled from it with loud railing, grew angry and unjust, and were on the way to become wicked.

It seemed to them worth any sacrifice, made at any cost, to obtain supremacy in an institution which, at the instigation of Miss Kimberley Finch, they had begun to claim as their own, because, as they said, their money was in it.

They had learnt to believe that no way was right except their way, which was her way; and saying that right must prevail, they had begun to sanction wrong. Moreover, they were half-educated; if, indeed, they could lay share to so large a fraction of the commodity; and were at the mercy of those members of their own sex represented by women like Miss Kimberley Finch. They had begun with a real, genuine, earnest desire for improvement, and had allowed themselves to be diverted from this aim by the love of power. They would have had quite as much power as they could desire if they had never heard of the lady from Grittleton; but she, as the champion of her sex, was by way of foisting them into all positions they could reach, and keeping them there, fit or unfit.

Miss Flint, the nominee and pet of the managing ladies, was pre-eminently unfit for her post.

Hard, unsympathetic, dogmatic, and stingy, her influence was that of a constant irritant to the best girls at the house. Some of them broke out into open insubordination, and were, according to the custom of all public schools, said Miss Kimberley Finch, summarily expelled, or they subsided into sullen indifference, like Nora Stewart.

The house was not a home. There was nothing homelike in it. Miss Ellen Green, of a warmer, kindlier nature than her colleagues, saw and regretted this. She asked the girls to tea with her, by twos and threes; loaded her table with pasties and fruit, spent the evening in showing them photographs of works of art which she had brought from almost every gallery in Europe, and sent them away with softened hearts and kindlier looks.

But a home atmosphere of distrust, suspicion, and secret antagonism prevailed against her weak efforts, and on no one had they produced such disastrous effects as on the Irish girl, Nora Stewart.

School life would have been a cruel ordeal to her under the most favourable circumstances.

She had been accustomed to run bare-headed about the fields and lanes near her home. It was a painful restriction to her to be compelled to wear a hat. She was a wild, bright, merry child, a great ignorant baby of seventeen, who was all at once treated as a responsible grown-up person. For a short time she was kept in awe by her companions and Miss Flint; then, as the fear of them wore away, and as she found herself lonely and without a friend, she tried to relieve the tedium of her life by a few foolish tricks. They were quite harmless in themselves, and might judiciously have been met, first of all with a laugh, and then with a protest on account of their childishness. But Miss Flint and the three ladies talked gravely and looked severe; Nora's companions were requested to communicate with her only on the subject of lessons, and the Irish girl, after some ineffectual outburst of passionate protest, subsided into dull indifference. Her final freak of dressing up a figure in the ladies' waiting-room had brought not only severe reproof, but punishment of a kind most galling to her. She was requested to keep her room, and was informed that she would not be allowed to join her companions, even at meal-times, until she had explained, to the satisfaction of the managing ladies, how she had become possessed of Miss Ravenshaw's umbrella.

It was in vain that Nora stated she had taken

it without even knowing to whom it belonged,
just as she had appropriated other articles that
suited her purpose.   Miss Flint had a deep-seated
jealousy of Miss Crayston.   The managing ladies
entertained bitter hostility towards her, and
wished to humiliate her through Bertie, since
they could not reach her more directly.

They had gradually talked themselves into a
condition in which they were no longer capable
of treating those whom they suspected with
justice.   They spoke of Miss Ravenshaw as if
she had been a criminal, and laid traps " to detect
her," and to induce Nora to incriminate her.

The result upon Nora was disastrous.   Afraid
of saying a word that might injure Bertie or
reflect upon Miss Crayston, she refused to answer
any questions put to her.   Indignant at being
suspected of untruth, and urged to confess, she
refused to leave her room and dine alone in the
hall ; refused to eat the food sent to her, and
gradually sank into a condition of sullen apathy.

She was roused from this by the sight of the
violets, by the interview with Bertie and the
Lady Resident, and by that pleasant secret meal
which Bertie had flung so promptly to her.   A
violent reaction followed, and a tempest of tears
and sobs alarmed not only all the boarders in the

house, but, being followed by prolonged fainting
fits throughout the night, caused Miss Flint to
inform the ladies that it was of no use to struggle
any longer against Nora's obstinacy; that it
would be better to remove all restrictions, and
allow her to resume her previous position in the
house and college.

Miss Ellen Green was troubled; she thought
Nora ill, and was laughed at by her two friends.
She invited the girl to spend a few days with her,
and received a churlish refusal from Nora, which
made her angry. Still she really had a kind
heart, or rather she had a nature which finds it
painful to witness suffering. She insisted on
delicacies being provided for Nora, whose appe-
tite seemed to have forsaken her; and had a fire
lighted in her bed-room on the cold spring days.
Nora did not appreciate the last-named act of
kindness, or, indeed, the first. She refused to eat
the food; threw up her window, saying she was
stifled, and left it wide open all night. The
result was a violent cold, followed by congestion
and inflammation of the lungs; the attack was
pronounced slight, but her recovery was slow
and partial.

Her parents, who lived in the north of Ireland,
were asked to fetch her home as soon as she was

convalescent, but they decided that she should remain at St. Mary's until the summer. Nora, who knew with what difficulty funds had been provided in order to give her two years at college, and prepare her, as it was hoped, to take a situation as governess, made no complaint of any kind with regard to this arrangement. Her letters home grew shorter and shorter, until they degenerated into formal notes; but there was decided improvement in the spelling, and Mrs. Stewart came to the conclusion that Nora was learning to write with a dictionary by her side, and that until this discipline was unnecessary much information must not be expected from her.

When Miss Ellen Green visited Nora she could not always resist the temptation to take Bertie with her. She had done so once because Bertie, waiting outside the door of the house, had asked so prettily and so urgently to be allowed to see Nora that Miss Ellen Green could not refuse. When she saw the delight of the sick girl, how meekly Nora received from Bertie instructions as to how and when she was to take all the good things that filled the little basket of the managing lady, how merry Nora could be and how bright and happy she could look, how cheerful Bertie was, though her eyes filled

with tears when she entered the sick room, all
these things made Miss Ellen Green waver. She
did not renounce allegiance to her friends, or go
so far as to assert that they were mistaken in
their estimate of Bertie's character and the influence of the Lady Resident; but she put the
whole question resolutely aside, and comforted
herself by arranging visits for Bertie whenever
she could do so.

At length Nora was able to leave her room:
she began to resume her attendance at the
classes, and even to take short walks on the
cliff. But when she had reached this stage
Bertie found it daily more difficult to obtain
access to her. Miss Ellen Green left Minster, and
then it became impossible.

The three managing ladies had received an
invitation from Miss Kimberley Finch to join
her in Oxford, and from thence to go with her
to Grittleton and take lodgings: "which would
make it possible to confer at length upon College
difficulties, and probably find a solution for
them." So wrote their adviser; and the Minster
ladies acquiesced.

"It is delightful to be without them:" said
Mrs. Brownlow, after they had been absent a
month; "but, dear Helen," and she threw her

arms round the neck of the Lady Resident, "it is a very good thing you are here, for this college is in a most awful muddle."

"How so?" inquired Miss Crayston, who was sitting at the window in her little parlour at St. Mary's.

"Why, there seems to be no money. The committee met on Monday, and the council met twice last week, and no one knows what to do."

"What has become of the fees?"

"Oh, they were divided as usual; but, you know, they amount to very little; and now there are tremendous bills for repairs and for the painting and stencilling of the staircase, which Miss Ellen Green insisted on getting done in an artistic manner, and there is no money to pay for anything."

"But there is the reserve fund:" urged Miss Crayston.

"No one can get at it. The chairman has tried, and the treasurer has tried, and I believe the whole council, individually and collectively, have tried. No one can touch it."

"What will be done?" asked Miss Crayston.

"Can't imagine. The Principal is very angry because the builders have dunned him, and the

Professors are furious because they have been
applied to for money by the decorators. Oh,
and the best of the joke is, that a Grittleton
solicitor has written on behalf of the managers,
to ask that the rent of St. Mary's may in future
be forwarded to him, and to suggest what he
calls an 'equitable arrangement' for the repay-
ment of the loan. When it came to that the
Principal telegraphed to Mrs. Armstrong, desiring
her to fix a day on which she could attend a
special meeting of the council."

"When will it take place?" asked the Lady
Resident.

"It is over. She telegraphed in answer that
it must be held in the course of two days, no
doubt expecting that this would be impossible;
but the Principal replied that he would receive
the council at the Abbey. She came down by
the night train, and is no doubt now on her way
back to Grittleton again."

"And how did the meeting pass off?"

"The men say they are very much amused,
but I think they are angry. Mrs. Armstrong
listened to all that was said, made no remarks,
collected the bills and dunning letters, put them
into her bag, and closed it with a snap that resounded through the room. Then she drew her

lips together, rose, said 'good morning,' and went
away."

"What does it mean?" asked Miss Crayston.

Mrs. Brownlow shrugged her shoulders:

"You will hear what Walmsley says:" she
replied. "And see, there is Goldworthy Fynes
coming up the road; we will ask what he
thinks."

Mr. Fynes joined the ladies with alacrity, and
seemed well-pleased to give his version of the
morning's meeting.

"Any scheme in which Lady Mary and Mrs.
Milner concur must be one that they conscientiously believe to be right, and they will doubt-
less influence Miss Julia Spiers:" remarked Miss
Crayston, when she had heard the report he
gave.

"We have nothing to do with the conscience
of these ladies:" replied Mr. Fynes with asperity;
"and if they make proposals that are objec-
tionable we shall not be at all more inclined to
accept them because they are conscientiously put
forward. A more important point is, whether
Lady Mary, Mrs. Milner, and Miss Spiers are
disposed to act independently. If they simply
succumb to the other ladies we shall be hard put
to it." .

"Do you attribute these pecuniary difficulties to the action of any individuals on the council?"

"Undoubtedly," replied the Professor; "and yesterday I assumed a very bold attitude with good effect. I recurred over and over again with considerable asperity to the subject of the reserve fund and the rent. Mrs. Armstrong protested that she did not intend to claim it. I did not, however, thank her, but contrived to shew a sense of injury that the smallest allusion should have been made to it by the Grittleton solicitor."

"My husband told me," said Mrs. Brownlow, looking at the Professor with frank simplicity, "that you did this with the most fearless courage. I was pleased to hear it, because I am sure it must be very difficult to shew a sense of injury when you are asked to pay a debt."

"Not at all:" replied the Professor, sharply. "It is a perfectly natural feeling. Moreover, under the management of these ladies St. Mary's has long been approaching a financial crisis which it has at last reached."

"Do you hold them responsible for our present condition?" asked Miss Crayston.

"If I was to say that they had deliberately brought about the present condition," replied Mr.

Fynes, "I should be alleging more than I have
the means of knowing. Of so much, however,
there can be no question, they have no motive
for shunning financial difficulties which will place
the institution at their mercy. I think I may go
a little further, and say that they have done their
best to cripple the institution in order that it
may be induced to surrender to them at dis-
cretion."

"I feel," said Mrs. Brownlow, rubbing her
hands slowly and gently, "as if I was sitting
with Guy Fawkes amongst whole barrels of
gun-powder."

The Professor looked keenly at her, and she
gazed upon him earnestly in return. He tossed
back his hair and continued :

"I believe I may also say that the majority of
the council are indignant at such a policy on the
part of ladies sitting with them at the council
board, and closely engaged in the every-day
management of the college."

"I should think so :" replied Mrs. Brownlow.
"In fact I believe I may go so far as to say, that
some of them are furious."

"I don't see any way out of the difficulty : "
said Miss Crayston, sighing.

"Don't take it too much to heart :" urged the

Professor : " If need be I think we shall threaten secession, and the establishment of a rival college ; though I very much doubt whether we could do it.   Of this not a word, because it is our last card, and must be played with caution."

" Cards ! " exclaimed Mrs. Brownlow.   " I see a glimpse of daylight.   We are playing what the Americans call the game of Brag.   Our opponents have enormous advantages, and we must make up for it by prudence and audacity, judiciously combined."

" Our majority is precarious : " said the Professor, shaking his head : " A compromise may be politic."

" No ; no compromise : " replied Mrs. Brownlow firmly.   " We fight to the bitter end, don't we, Miss Crayston ? "

But the Lady Resident looked grave.

" I don't understand," she said, " what has brought about so great a change in the respective attitude of the majority of the council and ladies who have done so much for the good of St. Mary's."

" Don't you know : " replied the Professor, rising and standing before her chair, " don't you know that since you have been here they have found it impossible to bring the whole institution

under their private and personal management.
You very properly refer all matters of importance
to the council, and I think you have found the
majority at all times disposed to approve of the
course and protect your independence.   If that
majority is ever forced to succumb it will not be
from disloyalty to you, but because the financial
pressure exercised by these ladies has left them
no choice."

The Professor left the room.   When the door
was closed Mrs. Brownlow exclaimed:

"I am too angry with that man.   He can
never send a fox into anybody's henroost without
tying a fire-brand to its tail.   As if it wouldn't
do enough mischief without that.   Don't let him
pose as your champion, Helen, whatever you do;
and don't let him persuade you that the fight is
raging round your standard, and that he alone is
willing to die in defence of it."

"But I am exceedingly sorry to hear that there
is so grave a difficulty.   It seems to me that
the very existence of St. Mary's is threatened."

"My husband is coming to fetch me after his
walk, and you shall hear his report.   Do you
know that 'I offered to chaperon Miss Flint the
other evening.   You should have seen the look
she gave me."

" May I ask the occasion of the offer ? "

" I saw her standing at the house door in the dusk as I was bringing the boy and his nurse back from the cliff. She looked too lugubrious. I thought a little fresh air would brighten her complexion, so I suggested that she should walk with me to the bower: ' It is far too late for a lady to be on the cliffs,' she said, with great severity. It was very impertinent, you know, as she saw I had come from thence ; so I replied : ' It *would* be considered peculiar if you were seen there alone ; but if I am with you no one can disapprove.' I assure you, dear, that John and I have had much fun out of that little adventure."

Miss Crayston smiled, but did not reply.

" Where is Bertie ? " asked Mrs. Brownlow.

" She has obtained permission to sit with Nora Stewart for an hour."

" Do you know that girl is very ill ? "

" So I fear : " replied Miss Crayston ; " but Miss Flint says it is really a case of hysteria. She kept a school for thirty years, and has had many cases of hysteria under her notice. Miss Ellen Green is very anxious, and she went with me to talk over the case with Miss Flint, who certainly at the time convinced us both that her view is correct : or rather, I ought to say, she showed us that she is, in her own way, doing everything that she considers desirable for Nora."

"I thought Bertie told me she was not allowed to see Nora ?"

"There was a difficulty about it at one time. Miss Flint complained that Bertie's visits made Nora hysterical, and that the girls discussed symptoms, and talked of absent friends. However, Miss Ellen Green has over-ruled all objections, and of course Bertie is too anxious about Nora to risk an allusion of any kind which may excite her. She will be extra-careful in choosing topics of conversation ; and if there is no ill result from the visit she is now paying they are to meet daily."

"Helen Crayston," said Mrs. Brownlow, emphatically, "Nora is no more hysterical than you or I. Something is wrong with her lungs or heart, and her friends ought to come and take her home."

"I saw a letter from Mrs. Stewart yesterday," continued Miss Crayston ; "Dr. Smart had, at the request of Miss Green, written to her, and this was her reply. She says that she has every confidence in Miss Flint, is sure Nora has even more care than she would receive at home ; Mrs.

Stewart has a young baby and cannot travel, nor can the father leave home until July. Ah, here is Bertie. Well, how did you find Nora?"

"As bright as a bird, and so pleased to see me. She has got a photograph of the new baby, such a darling. Her father is coming to take her home in the summer, and we talked about the children in our respective families, and had much fun over their ways and words."

"How does she look?" asked Mrs. Brownlow.

"Her face is rather thin, and that makes the eyes seem larger than they used to do. At first I thought their colour was changed from blue to black, but I see it is that the pupils are distended so that you see nothing else. She was breathless sometimes; but you know what a cough she has had. She complains of rheumatism in the left arm; it is rather painful sometimes, otherwise she is very well."

"Come, that is better than I had hoped:" exclaimed Miss Crayston.

"You think it sounds well?" asks Mrs. Brownlow, doubtfully. "Perhaps it does; and now, young people, I believe that my husband has either forgotten me or he is detained at Upton. I shall not wait any longer, or my boy will be late for his tea. He always sits up to the tea-

table with me in the afternoon ; and I want you
two to come and tell me if you think my son and
heir is doing pretty well."

"I met him in the Wilderness this morning,"
said Bertie, "and he made me take him out of
the perambulator and carry him to this door. I
assure you my arms ache now. He is as big and
heavy as a child of two years old."

"Bertie, you are a duck," exclaimed Mrs.
Brownlow, kissing her; "and you shall have
honey on your bread and butter. Do make haste
and get your bonnet, Miss Crayston. When any
one speaks of the boy it always makes me in a
fidget to get home to him."

CHAPTER XVI.

NORA GOES HOME.

"HAVE you seen Nora to-day?" asked the Lady Resident, three weeks after the events narrated in the last chapter.

"No; Miss Flint won't let me go to her room:" replied Bertie.

"The doctor has passed twice. I fear that he has been called in."

"I don't think Nora is ill:" urged Bertie with eagerness, unwilling to concede such a possibility. "It is Miss Flint's way. She can't help being gratuitously disagreeable, poor old thing."

"Bertie, you have quite a childish habit of saying 'poor old thing.'"

"I learnt it at home, you know; or at any rate I got it from home. Now that I have been so long away I begin to cling to the old familiar customs."

"I don't see why you should cling to this
one. You call all the ladies of whom you do not
approve 'old things.' It shows a want of re-
source ; you should enlarge your vocabulary."

"Ah, but you don't discriminate : " replied
Bertie, laughing. "Haven't you remarked that
I called Mrs. Armstrong a horrid old thing, and
somebody else a pitiful old thing ? I dare say it
is childish ; indeed, it is Ethel's expression. She
is my pet, you know, and when I say old thing
I see and even hear her. I believe I use her
very tones."

"It seems to me," replied Miss Crayston,
"that such a way of recalling your sister is like
looking at a bad photograph of her. As to Nora,
I fear she must be ill. She was at the literature
class last week, and I was quite shocked to see
the way she went up-stairs. She was obliged to
pause at every step, and even then she was
breathless before she reached the first floor."

"How cruel of her parents not to come for
her ! "

"That is a hasty judgment, Bertie. I wish
the parents were here ; but I doubt if Nora could
take a long and fatiguing journey."

" Do you think she is dangerously ill ? "

" Her state seems to me precarious, but I have

not Miss Flint's experience; and Miss Flint, as you know, is quite convinced there are no alarming symptoms."

"The managing ladies have returned:" said Bertie after a pause.

"Yes; I saw them last evening. Miss Green was here this morning: she says they are distressed at the great change they see in Nora, and she has written to urge one of the parents to come as soon as possible."

"I am very glad of that."

"I don't know that it will do much good, for Miss le Mesurier has also written to say she thinks there is no cause for alarm. By the way, Bertie, there is to be a grand entertainment a fortnight hence, on Whit Monday."

"Where? why?" exclaimed Bertie. "How awfully jolly!"

"Here, in the College; an evening party given by the managing ladies. All Minster is to be asked, or is asked already."

"How delightful!" said Bertie, dancing round the room; "but why is it on Whit Monday, just when we were to go to the Carters?"

"They will come to Minster, and we must postpone our visit. You see, the ladies had to decide on a day when the class-rooms were

not wanted ; and after Whit Monday there will
be no holiday until the summer vacation.   Mrs.
Brownlow has asked us to spend Monday and
Tuesday with her, so as to relieve Mrs. Gibson,
who seems oppressed at the prospect before her."

"She is wandering about the house in the
most melancholy manner; and just now, as she
opened the door for me, she said : ' Can you tell
me, miss, if there's such a thing as squerm
candles in Minster ; for I sez to Miss Flint, sez
I, taller won't do for the quality ; they're all very
well for the young ladies in the 'ouse, but the
quality must have squerm.'   I was so puzzled
that I could think of nothing to say in reply,
except that I'd ask you."

"Mrs. Gibson has been greatly excited the
whole morning : " said Miss Crayston.

"Of course the party will be postponed if
Nora is really ill ?"

"I don't know ; I think not.   The house and
the college are quite distinct.   I did refer to the
subject, but Miss le Mesurier says that the
greater part of the invitations are already sent
out."

Bertie was silent.   After a few moments she
said :

"Of course Nora will get better."

But Nora did not improve; day by day her strength failed, and at last the time came that she could no longer leave her bed. It was the Saturday preceding the day appointed for the college party, and Miss Crayston, who had retired late to rest, had fallen into an uneasy sleep, troubled by dreams of the sick girl, when she was roused by the voice of Mrs. Gibson :

"Will you please come to Miss Nora, mum; she's very bad."

"Have you told Miss Flint?"

"Lor', mum, why she've been with 'er all night."

"Did Miss Flint ask you to fetch me ?"

"Well, mum, if you *must* 'ave the truth, she did *not.*"

"Do you think I can be of any use ?"

"Well, I'll tell you ezackly 'ow it is: Miss Nora is that bad with a kind of spazzims that I raally do think as she'll die. Gibson has gone for the doctor, but it's very nigh two mile off, and doctors ain't easy roused; you see, 'e'll either be in his fust sleep, and then nobody can't wake a man, or else 'e'll be in 'is second, and then he sleeps 'eavy."

"Well!" said the Lady Resident, sitting up and looking at Mrs. Gibson.

" Well : " repeated the porter's wife, wiping her eyes : " Liza she come to me and says : ' Do, Mrs. Gibson,' says she, ' do, for 'eavins sake, come with me, for I'm frightened out of my life. There's Miss Nora a-dying, I do believe ; and there's the missis a-telling of her to show a little couridge and keep up her sperrits, and that she'll soon be better.' "

Miss Crayston rose, and, putting on a dressing-gown, passed through the door of communication between the college and the house, and followed Mrs. Gibson to Nora's room.

" Now, my dear child, sit up ; just make an effort and take this sal-volatile : " said Miss Flint, not unkindly, and in somewhat tremulous tones.

The Lady Resident stood silent for an instant, and then she advanced to Miss Flint :

" Have you any hot fomentations or mustard poultices ? I think they should be applied immediately."

" We are quite accustomed to these attacks : " replied Miss Flint, sharply ; " it will pass off very shortly. Now, my dear, do make an effort, just to please me."

" I don't think she is conscious : " urged the Lady Resident.

" Pray, Miss Crayston, spare me sentimental

exaggeration. Nora, my love, do try to attend to what I am saying. It's all for your own good."

The doctor's step was heard ascending the staircase. He entered the room and advanced to the bedside.

"What is to be done?" asked Miss Flint in great agitation, as she saw the doctor gravely watch his patient.

"Nothing:" he replied. "Nothing can be done."

"What do you mean?" she exclaimed.

"It will be over in a few minutes:" he continued, taking Miss Flint's hand and leading her away: "She is dying."

Miss Flint trembled violently and turned ashy pale.

"Impossible!" she said, sinking into a chair. "Shall I telegraph for her friends?"

"As you please. Any moment may be the last. Stay!" And once more he advanced to the bed and stooped over the dying girl; whilst Miss Crayston kneeled by her side, and, clasping the cold hand, followed Nora through the dark valley, and to the gates of death, with prayer.

"Nothing could have saved her:" said the doctor, half-an-hour later, as he and the Lady

Resident stood at the open window of an adjacent room. " I warned her friends some time ago that the next attack would probably prove fatal."

" Why have they left her here ?"

" A young baby in the house, measles, a mother who couldn't leave her children, and a father who couldn't get away from his office ; but the chief reason," continued the doctor with some bitterness, " is the medical knowledge that some ladies possess."

" Knowledge or ignorance ?" asked Miss Crayston.

" Well, well, one or the other. At any rate Mrs. Stewart wrote that she was sure her daughter was not ill, *because*— and she wrote twelve pages about somebody else's daughter; whilst Miss Flint was also sure, *because* she had known twenty-nine girls with hysteria."

" Was it hysteria ?"

" Nothing of the kind. It was disease of the heart. I told them so."

Dr. Smart left the house, and Miss Crayston stood looking out over the wilderness towards the green fields far away. Larks were rising in the sky. Their song was as the beating of wings. It seemed to the Lady Resident an aspiration as well as a hymn of triumph ; she thought of the young soul that had gone out into the brightness of the morning, and was winging its way—whither? And as she mused, the lark she had watched, that fluttered and paused, singing clear and strong as it rose higher and higher, suddenly ceased, dropped down out of the clouds, hovered an instant above a distant field, and settled upon the well-loved nest; and then the Lady Resident covered her face and wept.

She was roused after some time by a voice which said, not unkindly:

"I am sure it is very compassionate of you to feel so much for this poor girl." Looking up she saw Miss Ellen Green.

"We have been sent for," said that lady, wiping her eyes; "but it is too late. All was over when we arrived. However, we have the satisfaction of hearing from Dr. Smart that nothing more could have been done. Miss Flint is really invaluable, and her devotion to the College seems to increase, if that is possible. Will you come with me to the dining-room, Miss Crayston? we want to consult you with regard to a matter we have to take into consideration."

Miss Crayston followed, and found Mrs. Armstrong and Miss Flint sitting at a table, and Mrs.

Gibson, with red eyes and swollen face, carrying in a tray with tea, and bread and butter.

"You see," continued Mrs. Armstrong, who was speaking when they entered, and who shook hands in an absent manner with Miss Crayston, "you see that nothing can now affect the dear one we have lost. The dead are in every way beyond our reach, but the dear girls committed to us are a sacred charge. We must not allow their young lives to be blighted by the terror of death."

"I have known cases," said Miss Flint, "in which a delicate girl has never recovered from the sight of a corpse."

"Oh lor', mum," exclaimed Mrs. Gibson, with a fresh outburst of crying, "you did give me such a turn. To hear you speak like that of a corp, and poor Miss Nora; Oh, dear me! Oh dear, oh dear!"

Three of the ladies looked at each other with alarm as they heard the shrill sobs of the porter's wife; but Miss Crayston poured out a cup of tea, and saying:

"Now come with me, Mrs. Gibson; I am going to make you comfortable. You have been up all night, and are quite worn out." She led the way to the door.

"Sadly familiar with inferiors:" groaned Mrs. Armstrong.

"It is quite sickening:" exclaimed Miss Flint. "Neither Gibson nor his wife have a will of their own where she is concerned."

"In the present case that may be useful:" said Miss Ellen Green.

When the Lady Resident returned, Mrs. Armstrong spoke of the effect that Nora's death would produce upon her companions in the house.

"They will indeed miss her, and mourn for her:" replied Miss Crayston, to whom Mrs. Armstrong addressed herself. "She is very much beloved."

"Ah, that is not what I mean:" said Mrs. Armstrong, with characteristic hesitation. "You see—er—we want to save our young friends—er—from what is painful—er—gratuitously painful. In fact we must save them; it is a duty to save them."

"Death is terrible to the young, to us all," replied the Lady Resident, very gravely; "but I don't see how we can obliterate the terror that it inspires; and if we believe that life and death are both decreed by God, who loves us, I don't see why we should wish to be saved out of His hands."

" Pray, Miss Crayston, do for once try and take a sensible, practical view : " snapped Miss Flint.

Miss Crayston turned to the speaker and looked with that slight contraction of the brow which gave such earnest gravity to her expression.

Miss Ellen Green interposed :

" My dear Miss Flint ! No wonder you are overwrought with all that you have passed through ! I am sure Miss Crayston will agree with us, that it is impossible to leave a dead body in St. Mary's house, occupied as it is by our dear girls. We have therefore resolved to remove it to an unoccupied room which happens to be on the basement."

" Where ! " ejaculated Miss Crayston. " On the basement ! Do you mean that little dark room ? "

" My dear Miss Crayston," said Miss Ellen Green, in a soothing manner, " it is only for a day or two; and remember that the living are our charge. We must act up to our conscientious conviction of what is right for them."

Miss Crayston was silent. After a few moments she said :

" Will you allow the dear child to be moved to my room ? I shall receive it as a special favour if you consent; and I will prepare the room immediately."

Two of the ladies moved away, and there was a whispered conversation, the concluding sentence of which was : " It will be much better if any of the friends *should* come ; " and thereupon they returned to Nora's room, and the pale form was carried to Miss Crayston's bed.

An hour later Bertie was heard moving in her room, and singing as was her wont. The Lady Resident went to her, and gently told her all that had happened during the night. Bertie listened with a white, still face:

" I have never looked upon the dead : " she said, " may I go with you and see her ? "

" In an hour's time : " said the Lady Resident. " I should like to get some flowers after breakfast, and we will take them with us."

Bertie went out to the Principal's garden, and returned with a basket of white blossoms.

" The gardener will get better ones this afternoon," she said, " but these will do in the meantime."

Hand in hand Miss Crayston and Bertie entered the solemn chamber of death, and Bertie, kneeling down to gaze on the still face, said with streaming eyes :

" How beautiful she is ! How peaceful ! All the look of trouble and pain has vanished. Surely she is with God. Surely she is at peace and in perfect bliss, for her face is like the face of an angel. Oh, Nora, Nora, if I had only loved you better, and tried to help you more." And Bertie reverently kissed the pale hands, and smoothed the bright curly hair of the wild Irish girl.

"If we had known!" she exclaimed; "if we had been with her! Why my mother will sit up night after night with the poor lonely women of the village when they are dying! She would not have left you, Nora dear, as I have done."

"Bertie, we did not leave her. She knew that we loved her. She knows it now. It is God who decrees life and death and the manner of it. It is not in our hands. To Nora, death has come swiftly and peacefully. She knew none of the terror of it, but little of the suffering. She was conscious only of weakness, and looked forward to the summer and her return home without even undue longing for it."

"Yes; she talked so much about home of late," said Bertie, "and it was *this* home that was in store for her. Nora, dear Nora, good-bye, good-bye."

"Don't cry, my child:" said the Lady Resident.

"I will not:" said Bertie, clasping the hand held out to her. "God is in heaven. He has

ordained death for us, and for her; and see how
beautiful she is, more beautiful than when she
lived. I think God must give this beauty in
death that we may not be frightened at the
silence and the cold. You will write to her
friends, will you not? We will make her room
beautiful with flowers. They will see she was
beloved."

They moved gently and spoke low as Bertie's
skilful fingers arranged the flowers she had
brought with her, and disposed them in the room
and on the bed.

" They are not half lovely enough," said Bertie,
" and there is a tinge of colour, a kind of stain,
in these cyclamens. I want stephanotis, and
eucharis, and white azaleas, and arum lilies. Don't
you think we might drive over to Castle Stair?
Lord Ronald told me they would all be away for
two or three weeks. The gardener, no doubt,
would let us have all we want. You know how
many flowers Lady Joscelyn always brings us."

"Yes," replied Miss Crayston. " I will send
to the White Hart for a pony carriage, and we
will go at once. It is a long drive, but we can
be home by one o'clock."

They returned laden with flowers, and when
Mrs. Brownlow called early on Monday morning

Bertie led her to Nora's chamber. A white wreath lay at the dead girl's feet, a white cross upon her breast, and bunches of white flowers were ranged along each side of the bed.

"When will her friends come?" whispered Mrs. Brownlow.

"I don't know," replied Bertie, softly; "we have seen no one since the morning. We shall have fresh flowers to-morrow, and every day."

The little lady knelt by the side of the bed with clasped hands, then she kissed the brow of the dead girl, and returning to Miss Crayston, burst into passionate crying.

"Oh, my dear," she said, "only think of the mother that bore her. I thought I should have broken my heart. I did not dare to cry before the beautiful marble figure; but only think of the poor mother! How does a mother bear it when she sees her child lie cold and dead? And then to be away, not to know if she was soothed and comforted to the last, if human love led her to the terrible brink of the grave where the love of Christ would meet her."

"But she was helped through all her trouble, even if she did not know the hand that helped her. We must not mourn for her as if we could have done so much."

"No:" said Mrs. Brownlow, wiping her eyes; "but it is the mother in me that mourns. All about my heart are strings and cords that tighten and almost choke me as I think of Nora:" and she wept afresh. "Don't be angry with me for crying; I shall feel better after it."

After a few minutes she said,

"I want you two darlings to go home with me. You have done all that the tenderest love could devise, and now I want you to come with me. You both look ill and worn out. My dear Helen is like a ghost."

Bertie looked at the Lady Resident.

"Miss Crayston was up all Saturday night," she said, "and she had no sleep last night."

"I thought so; then come back with me to lunch. After that Helen shall lie down for two or three hours, and then we will drive to the sands, and make John and the boy go with us. You know you are to stay with me to-night."

"Ah, but that is changed now," said Bertie eagerly. "We will not stay out of the house now, will we?" and she appealed to Miss Crayston.

"Not unless the friends arrive:" replied that lady. "Mrs. Armstrong asked me if in that case

we would give up all our rooms, and I said that
we would."

"Certainly," said Bertie, "they have the first
claim to this sacred charge:" but she looked
disappointed.

The Lady Resident, wan and tired, found some
difficulty in walking to Mrs. Brownlow's. Once
there, and resting on a bed like a little soft
white nest, she slept for some hours, whilst Bertie
kept watch. Tea was ready when they entered
the drawing-room.

"You are to make a good tea," said Mrs.
Brownlow, "for the evenings are long and light.
John says we will have a long drive, and return
to supper."

Bertie looked at the Lady Resident.

"We should like to go to St. Mary's for half-
an-hour," she said.

Mr. Brownlow moved uneasily on his chair.

"I met Miss le Mesurier; she was on her way
here to see you:" he said. "I told her you were
with my wife. She said something about friends
coming, and that they would be much obliged
if you would stay away to-night."

"How strange!" exclaimed Bertie.

"Of course it is not the friends who wish
that:" said Mrs. Brownlow. "You may be sure

they would like you to be there, and then they
would know that some one had loved their child.
I shouldn't mind the message if I was you."

"I am not sure, my dear, that you are giving
good advice. There may be reasons for the
request that we do not know."

"Yes," said Miss Crayston; "and if the friends
are there it will not be necessary for us to go.
We shall do so chiefly to gratify our own
feelings. I think, Bertie, we will wait till to-
morrow morning."

"Very well:" replied Bertie with a sigh.

And so they drove to the shore; and the coachman received private orders from Mr. Brownlow
to avoid passing St. Mary's.

"I should like to have seen our windows:"
said Bertie.

Mrs. Brownlow was about to speak to the
coachman, but her husband, unobserved, pressed
her hand, and she was silent.

Early on the following morning Bertie entered
Miss Crayston's rooms.

"Do you think we may go to St. Mary's
before breakfast?" she said. "I have been
dreaming of Nora all night. I have been so
troubled. I think we ought to have stayed.
Will it tire you? Shall I go alone?"

"No; I have been expecting you for some time. I shall be ready in five minutes."

When they reached St. Mary's Mrs. Gibson was at the door, in sharp altercation with two men who had come with a van. The ladies entered, and Miss Crayston beheld long forms piled up in the hall, and Gibson in his shirt sleeves packing crates of china and glass, whilst chairs, tables, and pots of flowers were in confused heaps.

"What does it mean?" asked Miss Crayston, who had stood for a moment silent, and with a sickening fear creeping over her. "What does it mean?"

"Well, mum," said Mrs. Gibson, taking up the corner of her apron and speaking angrily, "they hadn't ought to come till nine o'clock, them was Mrs. Armstrong's orders; and then, says she, we shall be ready for the young ladies at ten. Gibson an' me 'ud have 'ad everything ready by nine; and here it is only seven."

"But what does it mean?" asked the Lady Resident, fixing her eyes on the porter's wife.

"Well, mum, I suppose you know as last night was the party?"

"The party!" And the Lady Resident sat down with a frightened look.

"Well, mum, you'll excuse me. I might have been sure it was all unbeknown to you. But here they was a-singin' and a-dancin', and a laughin' and goin' on, and that poor lamb——"

Hasty steps came flying down the stone stairs, and Bertie, who had gone up without taking notice of the confusion in the hall, exclaimed:

"Oh, Miss Crayston, they have taken her away. The room is empty. She is gone. No one is there. Oh what have they done? what have they done?"

"They brought a coffin, and they've a-put the coffin into a box, miss, and carried it to the railway station. They come at six last night."

Bertie gave a cry of horror as Mrs. Gibson, with angry emphasis, made this statement. She looked round, and for the first time noticed the things that had attracted Miss Crayston's attention when they entered. She hurried first into one room and then into another.

"And oh," she cried, "could they talk and laugh and sing the very day, the very first day! Could they forget her so soon!"

"Lor' bless you, Miss Bertie, now don't you run away with that there notion. Why nobody knows it, no more than you know'd about the party."

"I did know," sighed Bertie; "but I forgot. It would never have occurred to me that there would be a party."

"Well, you see, miss, they dared me and Gibson, they *dared* us, miss, to speak of it to mortal being. They was a-telegraphing all day long, and from what I can make out they've a-stopped the friends from coming here; and Jones the undertaker has gone with the "—she paused —"with *the box* to Bristol, and there them as belongs to the poor dear soul will arrive to-night from Belfast; and little they'll ever know of all as has happened."

Mrs. Gibson sniffed loudly, and her husband dropped a tumbler, which fell with a crash on the stone floor.

"Let us go to the station;" said Bertie hastily, lifting the flowers she had brought with her.

"For what purpose?" replied Miss Crayston. "We can do no more. Come with me to the garden."

"Does Mrs. Brownlow know?" asked Bertie.

"I think not; but Mr. Brownlow must have suspected."

"I cannot rest:" exclaimed Bertie, "I cannot sit still. It seems to me so wicked, so irreverent to the dead, so disrespectful to the living. Why have they not allowed all to share in the sorrow which was sent to all ? Is it those three ladies who have presumed to interfere when God has spoken to us ? "

"Hush, my child ; He speaks also in this."

" What will her friends think ? "

" They will be spared pain. They will never know."

"Do you wish to return to Mrs. Brownlow ? "

" I think not. We will stay here."

" Oh, thank you : " said Bertie.

Meanwhile all traces of the festivities were removed, and by ten o'clock the college was in order for the resumption of work.

END OF VOL. I.